GODDESS ASCENDING

GODS AND GUARDIANS

HEATHER HILDENBRAND

Goddess Ascending
© 2019 Heather Hildenbrand

ISBN 9781795053655

CHAPTER ONE

IT'S happening again. This time, in public. Water clogs my mouth and nose. I kick my feet and stroke upward with my head tipped up, desperate for air, but it's no use.   Everything around me is dark, and I'm convulsing. Dying.

I've been drowning for weeks.

The dreams come while I'm wide awake and nowhere near water. The current dream releases me, and I cough, clearing my lungs from the imaginary liquid as the nightmare fades.

Sitting up, I frown and climb back onto the bench in front of my local gym. Grass sticks to my sweaty yoga pants, and I idly brush it away while doing a quick scan of the area.

One of the women from my self-defense class stands several feet away, gawking at me. I flip my hair saucily and pretend her Krav Maga instructor didn't just have what undoubtedly looked like a nervous breakdown.

I run a hand through my tangled black hair and

focus on breathing. Oxygen always tastes better after one of my weirdo daymares. As the woman gives up staring and hurries to her car, I chase my shots of oxygen with a few sips of water.

Above me, the stars twinkle like little sparkly eyes, laughing down at me for my dramatic display. Like the damn stars don't have anything better to do than gawk at my awkwardness. . .

"Hey, partner," a familiar voice says just as a body drops onto the empty space beside me.

"Hey, Finn." Partner means partner in crime. However, Finn is typically getting me *out* of trouble rather than helping me get *into* it.

I offer a weak smile and note the way his cheeks are still flushed from playing my "victim" in our recent class.

"You okay?" he asks, studying me closely.

"Yeah, totally fine. Why?"

"You fell off the bench," Finn says, and I groan.

"You saw that?"

"El, everyone in the parking lot and half the lobby saw it." His voice is gentle but also full of laughter. Finn's been my friend long enough to know I'm a puzzle.

"Whatever, I just tripped."

Finn grins.

"You were sitting down."

"That's a thing. Tripping out of a chair," I say, but Finn shakes his head.

"At least you didn't break something. The water cooler still hasn't been replaced since you knocked it over last week."

I wince at the reminder, deeply relieved that Finn finds it amusing now instead of weird. A simple drink of water had turned into a full-on daymare, and I'd somehow drop-kicked the cooler, flooding the break room with five gallons of water. By the time I'd come to my senses, Finn had pinned me to the wall. Apparently, I'd been calling him a demon and trying to claw his eyes out.

Although Finn had been worried at the time, he'd covered for me with our manager. Blamed it on the equipment being faulty and even broke the water tower stand to prove it.

"You did good tonight," Finn says, rotating his ankle. "That last takedown left me sore."

"Really?" I ask, not sure whether to believe him but relieved for the change of subject.

"Really. You're getting stronger."

His brown eyes sparkle with something. Pride? Whatever it is, I don't miss the toned arm that dangles from the bench behind me or attractive slant of his brows or the way his hair spikes kind of crazily now that he's worked out. Finn's not hard to look at, but for the year we've been friends, there's been nothing romantic between us. And I've watched with fascination while he steers clear of the women who try for romance. I'm not sure why.

Finn is a lone wolf.

Then again, so am I.

"Seriously, though," he says, and his expression turns intense. "Are you okay?"

"I . . ." The drowning is still fresh enough that the fear makes me scowl. I'm an excellent swimmer with no past water traumas, so I'm pretty certain my brain is officially broken.

However, my mother's mental health wasn't exactly the most stable. And just like that, the thought of her sends a pang through my chest. Today's been hard enough, but I already know tomorrow will be much worse.

A car pulls to a stop at the curb.

"Elidi!" Aunt Aerina calls, sounding urgent. She's always in a hurry.

"I'm fine," I assure Finn. "See you later." I jump up and hurry over to the Prius.

"How'd it go, sunshine?" Aerina asks, turning down her music.

Aerina has always called me sunshine. Just like Mom did.

In answer to her question, I wince, and Aerina cringes.

"That good, huh?"

"Class went great. Finn said he's actually sore from the last takedown demonstration I did."

"That's great. So what's—"

"I had the nightmare again. Or daymare. Or whatever it is." I blow out a breath.

Her smile falls.

"Oh." She signals then pulls the Prius away from the curb and heads for home. "I was really hoping that increasing your workouts would help center you," she says quietly.

"I think they're making it worse. Like my physical exhaustion is making me crazy or something. Or maybe it's genetic."

Aerina cuts me a look, and I know we're descending into a very familiar argument.

"Knowing how to defend yourself is crucial information."

"That's not what I—"

"And your genetics have zero insanity," she snaps.

Damn. I've struck a nerve.

"Your family tree is full of strong women, physically and mentally," she goes on.

"What about my dad?" I ask.

"What about him?"

"You don't know who he is, so we don't know what I got from his side of the gene pool." I shrug. "Maybe he's a psycho with delusions, and I'm just taking after him."

"Your father is not a psycho," she says firmly.

So firmly that she sounds . . . certain.

"Aerina, what do you know about him?"

She blinks, her gaze fastened firmly on the road ahead. "Nothing."

Her foot pushes heavier on the gas, and I try not to let my nerves show as she navigates the Prius along the winding roads outside our tiny town of Bridgeport, Washington. Instead of the skyscrapers and smog of L.A., what lies ahead are miles and miles of the Olympic National Forest and clean, clear oxygen and our fixer-upper farmhouse in the middle of nowhere.

Mom would have hated it.

"Your shtick is getting old," I say when the silence stretches and the road straightens again.

"I don't have a shtick."

I roll my eyes. "Please. Since Mom died, you've

done nothing but boss me around. Where we live, where I work—"

"Your work is good for you. L.A. wasn't safe anymore."

"Right. Muggers and carjackers," I say, repeating the tired story she keeps trying to feed me about my mother's mysterious death. "All you do is try to convince me of the danger we're in. Maybe that's why I'm having hallucinations of my own death."

"Don't be a smartass."

I know Aerina's losing her patience. Guilt pricks at me as I realize I'm not the only one in pain today. This is a hard week for us both.

I sigh. "I'm sorry. I just feel like I'm losing it, and I miss her."

Aerina's golden blonde hair and pink cheeks are gorgeous as ever, but it's a sad beauty now.

"I miss her too," she says quietly. "But don't give up, Elidi. Your birthday is coming."

I frown. "What does my birthday have to do with crazy daydreams about dying?" Instead of offering me an answer, she focuses on the road. Whatever. Aerina's always saying cryptic things to me about my daymares, and it's only gotten worse since Mom died.

She pulls into the driveway and cuts the engine, plunging the yard and porch into inky darkness.

Neither of us moves. I hate the dark.

Aerina turns and reaches for my hand.

"Elidi, we need to talk. There are some things you need to know about who you really are."

"What do you mean? Like about Mom?" I ask.

Aerina nods. "That's part of it. But there's more,

and I think it's time you know the truth. Come inside. I'll make some tea." She climbs out and adds, "We're going to need it" under her breath.

I step outside, and the chilly air lifts goose bumps along my arms. The loose leaves whisper against each other in the wind, and I have to force myself to reach back into the car for my gym bag rather than scurry after Aerina.

By the time I sling my bag over my shoulder and slam the car door shut, Aerina's already inside, and I'm alone.

"Be cool," I whisper to myself. "It's just the dark." I scan the pockets of shadows that line our yard. There is a border of trees out there, but right now, I can't even make out their silhouette.

"Just the night. There's nothing here that can—"

A pair of glowing red eyes materializes on my left, and I freeze. My throat closes, robbing me of the ability to scream.

The disembodied eyes begin to float closer. Just when I'm ready to admit the whole thing's some weird, wild creation of my own nightmarish imagination, a snout appears underneath the eyes. The thin lips attached to the end of it open, and an inhuman scream splits the air.

From deep within the forest, a howl goes up. It's nearly lost to the deafening screech coming from the creature.

The red-eyed monster floats closer, allowing me a look at its enormous four-legged body. It looks like some kind of giant horse that breathes steam from its nostrils. My panic turns to desperation. My training kicks in. Self-defense is all about being the first to act.

My legs lurch forward, and then I'm running up the porch steps and into the house. The screen door bangs loudly against the frame.

"Aerina!" I'm terrified the monster will follow me inside. My feet don't stop moving. I run toward the kitchen and stop short of plowing into her.

Aerina's eyes are wide and panicked. "What is it?"

"Something . . . outside." I'm starting to shake, and the thing outside lets out another deafening scream. I cringe.

"What is it?"

She frowns, vaguely worried, but otherwise she looks unaware of the screeching monster in our front yard. How can she not hear that?

"Can't you hear it?" I ask.

"I don't hear anything. What does it sound like?"

"Like a freaking migraine waiting to happen."

"What did you see?" she demands.

"I saw glowing eyes, and then—"

Another scream rents the air, this time closer. Inside.

Aerina's eyes bulge, and she drops the kettle I hadn't noticed. Good. She can hear it now.

"Upstairs," she snaps. "Quickly."

I'm already running and take the steps two at a time with Aerina urging me to go faster from behind. My toe catches on the top stair, and I stumble upward. Aerina barely manages to keep from falling on top of me.

With my forehead throbbing where it smacked the floor, a wave of dizziness washes over me, and my vision blurs.

Below, the screaming continues.

"How the hell did they find us?" Aerina mutters. She sounds more worried than I've ever heard her before—aside from the night Mom died.

"What?" I ask, but my words are lost in the wailing that now shakes the pictures on the walls.

Aerina jumps up and yanks me to my feet.

I scramble onto the landing.

"In here!" Aerina holds the door to her bedroom open, and I dash inside.

Her antique dresser, opposite the neatly made bed, holds a collection of crystals that form a circle.

Aerina points to the arrangement.

"Take the prism," she says. "Don't let go of it."

She flips up the rug in the center of the floor, exposing a strange chalk-etched symbol on the hardwood.

I grab the crystal from the center of the arrangement, and she shoves me into the center of the floor art.

"Don't move," she orders me, running back to the door.

Something crashes downstairs.

I squeeze the bluish crystal in my hands, and Aerina steps into the hall. Her normally blue eyes are nearly gray and wide with panic.

"Elidi, I mean it. Stay inside the protection rune. No matter what you hear." Her voice wobbles, and she looks afraid.

Aerina is never afraid.

Panic spears through me, sending my stomach

roiling. What the hell is a protection rune? I look down at the drawing at my feet. When I look up, Aerina is closing the door.

"Wait! What are you doing?"

"I love you, Elidi. Hemera loved you, too. I know you'll make us proud. You're the light. The sunshine. Remember that."

"What are you talking about? We need to call the police. Get in here before that thing—"

She slams the door, sealing me in and her out.

I leave the circle and grab at the knob, but it's so hot it burns me. I jerk back in surprised pain. How the hell had it gotten so hot?

From the other side, the beast's scream turns to a high-pitched keening. The sound shakes the glass in the window until I'm afraid it'll shatter.

Aerina shouts something that I can't make out. The floors and walls begin to shake now too. Photo frames rattle then fall, shattering at my feet. I back away from the door and stumble back inside the chalk circle.

Outside, thunder rolls, and lightning splits the darkness, and my gaze flies to the window to my left.

In the glow of the lightning bolt, I see something run from the woods. A wolf a size unlike any I've ever seen. So large, it cannot possibly be real. As if it can sense me, or maybe sense my disbelief, it suddenly looks up, and our eyes meet.

Then the light vanishes, and the wolf is gone.

In the hallway, the screaming reaches a crescendo. Aerina is yelling words in another language, and more thunder rumbles the sky.

I run to the door and bang on it with my fists, too

scared to go for the knob again but desperate to save my aunt. The scream reaches a pitch I didn't think possible, and behind me, the window finally shatters.

The shrieking presses into me, eating at my sanity. I fall to my knees, covering my ears. I feel my grip on sanity slipping.

The sensation of water surrounds me. I gasp and clutch at my throat, forgetting the crystal. The prism falls from my hand and hits the floor.

Everything goes quiet—including Aerina.

My nightmare recedes, and as my vision clears, I straighten and inhale deeply.

My eyes swing from the jagged glass of the broken window to the closed bedroom door. I bite my lip until the taste of blood coats my tongue.

In the wake of the chaos, the stillness is just as terrifying.

Barely breathing, I touch a tentative finger to the brass knob. Then two. It's cool to the touch. I wrap my burned palm around the knob and twist.

The door creaks open, and something heavy thuds to the floor. I scramble backward, startled.

Through the cracked opening, I see a rectangular, gray stone. A red stain coats the side, and my breath catches as I realize what it is.

Blood.

My heart thunders in my chest.

Before I can dissolve into a puddle of fear, I swing the door wide and scoop up the stone. It's wet and sticky in my hand.

I do a quick scan of the hallway, but it's empty.

"Aerina?" I whisper.

Nothing.

Tiptoeing to the top of the stairs, I peer down to the first floor. The lights are off, but the moonlight from the windows offers just enough light for me to make out the empty living room.

"Aerina?" I say again.

No answer.

My legs wobble all the way down the stairs and through the living room. I find the kitchen empty too.

The back door bangs open, and I race through the dining room in time to see a flash of golden hair before it disappears into the night.

"Wait!"

I race to the open doorway only to stop short when a red-eyed beast steps into view. It looms way too close and is coming at me way too fast.

I scramble backward and bump into something behind me. My free hand touches heaving fur, and I jerk away with nowhere to run.

The red-eyed monster's gaze shifts from me to whatever's pressing in behind me.

The stone in my hand grows warm then hot.

"Elidi, don't open—" Aerina's voice stabs through the silence then cuts short.

I peer around the beast's shoulders in time to see a hand appear out of thin air. It wraps around Aerina's wrist and yanks hard. She loses her balance and begins to fall, but she doesn't make it to the ground before she's swallowed up into some sort of black hole.

The grass where she stood is blackened and smoking, but Aerina is gone.

I'm alone.

The beast before me screeches, squeezing into the doorway.

Panic claws at me, and my mind screams for me to run. I turn and trip, having forgotten the furry presence. My face connects with the floor, and the beast shrieks. When I roll over and open my eyes, a large wolf stares down at me.

The wolf shoves me with its nose, and I scramble up, stumbling toward the living room. Behind me, the beast in the doorway bellows in frustration and wiggles against the creaking wood.

The front door bangs open, revealing a second red-eyed creature.

I jump backward, and the stone falls out of my hand. The edge of it catches on the coffee table, and the rectangular stone springs open, becoming a box.

From inside, something dark leaps out straight at me. Before it can land, the wolf leaps, knocking me sideways. My head hits the floor, and everything swirls above me. Something lands on my shoulder with enough force that I scream. I look down and see a dark liquid swirling toward my chest. My skin burns as the liquid burrows through it and inside me. I curl against the wolf, clutching my stomach as the burning grows hotter, spreading over my hip.

The beast at the front retreats to get a running start at the door. The force of its momentum sends it crashing through the narrow doorframe.

The wolf scrambles off me and sinks its teeth into the monster's front leg. The horse-beast screams so loudly I clutch my ears and close my eyes. However, the worst of the agony emanates from the burning in my chest. Whatever that stone contained, it feels like it's poisoning me from the inside.

Then, suddenly, everything stops.

The screaming dies. The pain recedes.

When I open my eyes, the red-eyed monsters are gone, and my living room is destroyed.

I lift my head, and something moves near the front door.

The wolf I'd spied from the window earlier. And, it is as huge as I'd imagined it and with thick fur the color of vanilla cream.

Our eyes meet, and the wolf stares unwaveringly back at me.

In that small space lies every single possible future my life contains. I see stars and suns and moons—and death. Lots and lots of death. But I also see love. The kind that moves mountains and melts, well, panties. The kind I'd always thought only existed in movies.

It's the damnedest, craziest, wildest moment of my entire life. Including any of the psycho daymares that have knocked me off park benches.

Warm breath hits my face thanks to its half-open mouth, and I blink through my tears, certain I'm seeing some sort of panic-induced illusion.

"Am I dead? Because this is crazy, and I think it makes way more sense that I'm dead and you're . . . an angel?" I cock my head because that doesn't quite make sense either.

The beast's eyes widen, and I could swear it quirks a brow at me.

Outside, the rushing of the wind turns into what sounds like the beating of wings. The wolf's eyes narrow as it glances at the open door. Before I can ask any more questions about my entry into the afterlife, a voice rings out in my head.

If you want to avoid the same fate as your aunt, we have to go. Now.

I shriek and scramble backward into the corner underneath the bar counter that separates the living room from the kitchen. A stool topples over next to me, crashing loudly between us, and the wolf huffs.

Its eyes lock onto mine. *I know you hear me. Listen, we have to go. They're almost here.*

Outside, the sound of wings grows louder, and I realize whoever "they" are, the voice in my head is right. They're getting closer. And after the craziness I've witnessed so far, dead or not, I don't want to be here to meet them. But I'm also not going to go anywhere with a giant, telepathic wolf.

"Stay back," I yell, but my words are nearly lost over the sound of what can only be hoofbeats. On my roof.

The pain in my chest returns with a pang, and I notice for the first time that the wolf has a matching black spot on his own chest. What the hell was in that stone?

The wolf huffs with impatience and starts walking toward me.

This time, rather than retreat, I bolt. Or I try to.

I straighten too quickly, and the top of my already-bruised head hits the underside of the bar—hard. Pain shoots from the top of my head straight down to my toes. The world spins then tilts, and I lean way too hard to the right.

I go down swinging. My fist brushes along thick fur, and the last thing I see before I'm dragged under is a flash of white light shooting out from my own hand.

CHAPTER TWO

"MISS? Miss, can you hear me?"

I gasp, inhaling frantically as if I've been underwater again, and open my eyes. I look around with wild, jerky movements.

"Miss?"

"I hear you."

The living room is destroyed. The coffee table is in splinters with a large chunk of it sticking out of the couch which is upturned against the far wall. The barstool is charred and smoking lightly at my feet. The front door is completely gone. So is the enormous wolf.

"Where are your parents?"

I try to focus on the man kneeling before me. He's not alone. Two more strangers—one man, one woman, in matching jackets—walk into the house. Paramedics.

"Were you alone?" he asks.

I remember Aerina being sucked away into thin air. She's gone. I am alone.

"My aunt's not here," I say.

"Where did she go?" he asks.

An invisible fist grips my heart and squeezes as I remember Aerina's last words to me.

"No one else is home," the female paramedic announces as she reappears from upstairs. "Upstairs window is shattered, and the place is a mess just like down here."

I start to shake, and the man covers me with a blanket.

"What happened here?" he asks, leaning in close to hold my gaze.

"Something was in the house," I say. "Something loud."

"Loud how?" he asks. "What kind of noise did it make?"

"Screaming. The sound broke the window."

"Is that how it got inside? The window?" the man asks.

I shake my head.

"Door was wide open, sir," the male paramedic says.

"Door's in the yard," the female paramedic adds.

"No forced entry?" I look up at the new voice. A police officer stands by the door, looking at the remains of my home.

"Miss? What is your name?" the paramedic kneeling beside me asks.

"Her name is Elidi." The sound of my name coming from a familiar voice is like a lifeline to me.

"Finn?"

I scramble away from the paramedic, racing across the glass-strewn floor. Finn opens his arms and catches me in his strong embrace. His hands stroke over my messy hair. I bury myself against his flannel and squeeze my eyes shut, shaking and crying.

"Elidi," Finn says quietly against my ear.

In his arms, some of the panic melts away. I'm not completely alone.

"You guys go to school together or something?" I hear the officer ask.

"Her name is Elidi Brant. She's homeschooled. I live down the road. Came to check on her when I heard the sirens."

"Do you know what happened here?" the officer asks.

There's a pause, and I know Finn's finally taking in the destruction. "Mother of . . . What happened, El?" he asks.

"Someone broke in," I say. The words don't begin to cover what happened, but they're the closest thing I can say that anyone would believe.

From the yard, an engine shuts off, and car doors slam. I glance out the open door, and my eyes widen at the sight of all the emergency vehicles parked out front. Two ambulances, three police cars, and a fire truck light up the night sky in bright red, white, and blue strobe patterns.

"Who called you?" I ask.

"We got an anonymous tip there was a home invasion," he answers uncertainly. "It wasn't you?"

I frown, a few more tears leaking out without my permission. "No. I was busy trying not to get killed."

"We'll need a statement," the officer says quietly.

Finn nods. "Of course. Give us a moment."

Finn switches his hold on me, scooping me up and

carrying me around the corner and into the dining room. He sets me down gently in one of the dining room chairs then kneels in front of me.

The back door is closed and looks deceivingly untouched. I wonder if maybe I imagined the horse-monster trying to fit through the narrow frame, its red eyes glowing and breath puffing from its angry snout. Maybe Aerina's fine. Just out for a jog or donuts or—

"Look at me, El."

I look at Finn. His brown eyes stare steadily back at me.

"Tell me what happened," he says.

His voice is clear, free from any trace of suspicion or disbelief. And just like that, the grief hits.

My bottom lip trembles with the effort to keep from breaking down. My cold hands turn clammy, but I reach for Finn anyway, desperate to keep him from leaving. I can't lose him too. He's all I have left.

"Don't leave me," I say, and my voice breaks.

"I'm not going anywhere," he promises me. His honey-brown eyes swim with worry, but there's a sort of unshakeable confidence in Finn that I've always admired and that I desperately want to borrow now. "I just wanted to give you some breathing room. It's crowded in there."

I nod, unable to trust my voice. What would I do without Finn? Especially now?

"Where is Aerina, El?"

"She's gone," I whisper, and tears spill instantly down my cheeks.

"What happened?" Finn whispers back. His hands are warm on my knees, and I lean in, wanting to soak up more of the comfort his solid presence offers.

"I don't know. There was something here when we got home. It followed us inside, and it was screaming so loud. Aerina gave me a crystal and told me to stand inside the symbol."

"What symbol?" he asks.

"A star or something? It's in her room. I—I couldn't stay there. Not when she was down here with *it*." My voice breaks again. More tears fall.

I sniffle, and Finn's hands rub up and down against my leggings. Reassurance. I'm not alone.

"Did you see it?" he asks.

"I saw red eyes. It sounds crazy, I know, but—"

"Not crazy. Different," he says in a voice I've never heard him use before. "Did Aerina say anything before she left?"

I cock my head. "She didn't leave, Finn. She was taken."

"Of course. That's what I meant." He shakes his head. "Did she say anything else?"

"She locked me in the bedroom. The knob was hot, and I . . ." I blink, my memory flitting from one moment to another. "She said I was the light and that she loved me."

"How did you get out if the knob was so hot?"

"I . . . I waited, and then it just cooled." I frown. "What does that have to do with anything?"

He shrugs. "I just want to understand. You've been through a lot."

I nod. Of course. He's right. But something about his questions still bothers me. And then I realize something unusual.

The symbol. He didn't even ask what it looked like. Or what Aerina could have meant by calling me the light.

Through the haze of grief, I realize he's not asking any of the questions I would have expected. He's not nearly as confused as I would be. As I am.

I wonder what he'd say if I told him about the wolf who'd shown up to protect me. About the inky poison inside the broken stone and how it knocked us both across the room before soaking right into my skin without a scratch or stain. Or about the flash of light that shot from my own hand just before I passed out.

"What did the monsters look like?" Finn asks again.

This time, I hesitate. Some small voice in my mind whispers a warning, and I listen. Even though I hate the suspicion growing like a third wheel between us, I pretend.

Pressing my lips together, I shake my head. "Aerina's all I had Finn. The only family left. What am I going to do now?"

Something dangerous and foreign flashes in Finn's eyes. Something I've never seen from him before. It's slippery and gone before I can catch hold of what it all means.

Finally, he blows out a breath and runs a hand through his dirty blond hair. His eyes do a scan of the room, but I already know he's not seeing anything here. He's thinking ahead. Finn always does.

"It's going to be okay, El. Listen, the cops need to know what you told me. I need to tell them to check the upstairs bedrooms. I'm just going to pass on the information, and then I'll be right back. They'll want to hear it from you directly though. I need you to tell them, okay? Can you do that?"

His eyes are soft and so Finn-like that I tell myself I imagined any weirdness.

"Sure," I say. For Aerina.

"Good girl." He pushes to his feet then drops a quick kiss to the top of my head before turning for the door. "Don't move. I'll be right back."

Before he can get two steps, the officer appears, and I know without a shadow of a doubt he's heard every word we've just said. Finn glares at him, and I know he's just as pissed as I am about it. But he relays my story and then stands beside me while I repeat it one more time.

Then, things begin to move more slowly.

The officer disappears to check the bedroom.

He returns with more questions though none of them involve a weird symbol, and I do my best to answer. One by one, two more officers and the paramedic from earlier come visit me in the dining room with questions of their own.

Thanks to Finn's digging around, Aerina's photo is provided and will run on the evening news as a missing person. It's very surreal.

One of the paramedics examines me. I'm cleared, and they leave.

A social worker arrives. As a minor by only a couple of months, it's required.

More questions are asked.

Through it all, Finn remains glued to me, and the weight of his hand on my shoulder keeps me grounded.

I cry—a lot. But I also manage to answer every question they ask. Finally, the police give up on trying to get me to remember any more details, and they leave. Only Finn and the social worker, Amy-something, remain.

"Finn, do you think you could put some clothes in a bag for Elidi?" Amy asks.

I'm jolted out of my reverie and into the conversation as I realize she's trying to make him leave the room. "A bag?" I repeat, trying to think through the fog.

"You can come back for more when we have a more permanent place for you," she says almost like an apology.

"Where am I going?" I ask.

Amy's expression falls. "You'll have to stay at Ferndale House until we figure this all out," she says.

"Ferndale House?"

"I went over it with you a few minutes ago."

"Oh." My brain is fuzzy.

Amy looks up at Finn who is like a sentry on my left. His hand rubs slow circles into my shoulder blade as she tells him, "Elidi will need enough for two or three days. Can you pack that for her?"

Rather than answer her, Finn drops into a crouch beside me. "El?" he asks, his honey-brown gaze searching mine. "Will you be all right without me?"

I open my mouth to tell him no, but he beats me to it, adding, "Look. Through the window. The sun is coming up."

I look over, and sure enough, the sky is lightening to a soft gray with tinges of pink showing through the bare trees.

He turns back to me. "Two minutes," he promises.

At the sight of the sunrise, something inside me uncurls a little, and I exhale, nodding. "Okay."

Finn rises and steps past me on near-silent feet despite his heavy boots. I look back at Amy in time to see her attempt a smile. It's tired and fake, and I offer her nothing in return. My insides are still panicking at the realization I've lost the only family I had left in the world—and maybe my sanity too.

"It's going to be all right," Amy says, but her promise is as empty as her smile.

"Is the lie part of your protocol or just your own personal touch?" I ask dully.

Her smile slips. "Excuse me?"

"The lie," I repeat. "You don't know me or my life. I just lost the only living relative I have, and I am about to go live in a home with a bunch of other kids who also have nothing left to live for. How is it going to be all right?"

"Well, I . . ." She looks down, adjusting the papers in her lap, then looks back up at me. "I just think everything will work out for you."

I snort. "If you think that, you're more naïve than I am."

"Elidi, you're going through something horrible, but life never stays one way for long," she says. "Trust me. This won't last. Life will change. It will be okay."

I sigh, staring down at a spot on the floor. "Whatever."

Amy uncrosses and re-crosses her legs, leaning forward. "Elidi, I want to ask you while we're alone . . ." Something in Amy's tone catches my attention, and I look back at her, wary now. "Your friend. Finn. Is he—You feel safe with him, right?"

"Yeah. Why?" I ask slowly.

Her smile is back, tighter this time. More forced. "He's asked that you be placed with him until your birthday, and I just want to make sure he's someone you trust."

"Of course. I trust Finn with my life."

"Has he asked you to live with him before?"

"What?" I shake my head. "No. Why would he—?"

"I just want to make sure he hasn't been pressuring you to move out and be with him. I understand that dating an older guy, especially when you're homeschooled, can be—"

"Whoa, lady." I hold up a hand and straighten in my chair as understanding finally dawns. "Finn and I are just friends."

"I see. I assumed . . ." She forces another fake smile. "He seems very attentive." Even with my denial, she looks unconvinced. Nonetheless, she looks down and makes a note on her clipboard, and I have to fight the urge to reach over and break the damn thing over her head.

Was she really suggesting Finn might have hurt Aerina just to get his minor girlfriend to move in with him?

"He's a *friend*," I repeat through clenched teeth, "who is trying to comfort me after my aunt was attacked and taken against her will. I'd say *attentive* is more than appropriate considering the circumstances."

"Right. Of course." Amy writes something else down, and I grip the armrest until my knuckles turn white.

"Can I stay with Finn then?" I ask when the silence stretches. "Tonight?"

Amy looks up, startled. "Oh, no. Sorry, any requests will need to be processed through the proper channels. I'll submit the paperwork tomorrow." She glances out the window which now reveals a sky bright pink with the coming day. "Today," she corrects. "But it will still take at least seven to ten business days, and Finn will have to complete a full character and background check, not to mention we'll need to find out what you plan to do with your future."

"I've basically graduated," I tell her. "In the fall, I plan to enroll at community college and use it to get into a state school next year."

Amy smiles politely, either unimpressed or unconvinced. "That sounds great, but we'll need to take official statements from Finn and from both of your employers. Not to mention sending off for some sort of academic records for you. In the meantime, you'll be staying at Ferndale House, I'm afraid."

I drop against the back of the chair, feeling defeated all over again.

A pair of boots sound just outside the room, and a second later, Finn reappears. He's carrying my duffel in one hand and my shoes in the other. I don't even remember taking them off. "El, we need to talk about your organizational skills," he says, and I snort.

"We can talk about it, sure," I tell him.

He gives me a stern look, but I know it's only his way of distracting me. "Good. It's called an intervention, and your closet needs one."

I roll my eyes as he drops my shoes in front of me and I slide them on. When I'm done, Finn is waiting with my jacket, and I let him hold it for me while I stand up and slide it on. Amy stands too, her gaze watchful and obviously still not buying my "just friends" story.

"So?" Finn asks her. "What's the verdict? Can El stay with me for now?"

Amy flicks a glance at me then back to him before shaking her head and repeating the story she gave me. Finn's expression hardens, and by the time she's done, he finally looks pissed for the first time since walking in the door hours ago.

"El can't stay in a place like that," he says quietly.

"I'm afraid she doesn't have a choice right now," Amy says.

"You don't understand. She can't . . . It's not . . . What are her other options?" he asks.

"Finn." I slide my hand into his, mostly to diffuse his suddenly-boiling temper. I've never seen him get angry before. It's one of the reasons we're such good friends. A balance. He's water; I'm fire. Or that's what Aunt Aerina says. Used to say. Shit.

Where are you, Aerina?

My eyes once again fill with tears I'd assumed had already dried up hours ago. My hand in Finn's tightens, and he turns to look at me.

"I'll just go with her," I tell him quietly.

He nods, probably more silenced from the sight of my tears than my quiet declaration. Amy is quiet too and simply falls into step toward the front door, leading our processional.

Finn sighs, his shoulders sagging heavily. Then he wraps his arms around me and pulls me in for a tight hug. His hands smooth my hair, and he kisses the top of my head.

"I won't be far, okay?" he whispers. "Just be careful."

"I will," I tell him.

With one last hug, I'm out the door and on my way to the next chapter of my new life. The life of Elidi Brant, ward of the state.

CHAPTER THREE

EVERYTHING good in my life is gone.

Through the thin walls, I can hear yelling over the thumping music. No one at Ferndale House is friendly. Their definitions of friendship vary from wanting to trade drugs to wanting to trade sexual favors. I've made it clear I don't want friends like that or at all. But the word is out that the state-appointed therapist has prescribed me Xanax for the daymares, which she's labeled panic attacks.

My thoughts drift over the events of the last seventy-two hours, lazy and lulled by the pill I finally caved and took earlier. It's done its job, numbing the pain.

Despite her photo being plastered all over the news, there's no trace of Aerina. She's just gone. Her status as a missing person has become official, which means I'm a ward of the state now with paperwork to prove it. Amy-the-bitch texted me that news this morning. It's what pushed me to take the Xanax.

I'm officially an orphan.

Finn has called me twice today, but I haven't been able to bring myself to answer. He still isn't cleared to take guardianship of me by the state or allowed to visit me either.

Beside me, my phone buzzes again. I look down and see Finn's name on the screen and sigh again as I click to read his text.

If you don't call me soon, I'm coming over.

My stomach tightens at that. If Finn shows up, he'll take one look at this place and carry me away. And that won't bode well for his application. Amy's already warned me about funny business. She obviously still thinks Finn and I are a couple. I've given up trying to convince her differently.

Forcing myself to sit up, I dial Finn.

When Finn answers, his voice is overshadowed by the rapper boasting about "screwin' these hoes."

"Hello?" Finn says. "El? Is that you?"

"Hey, Finn." My voice is scratchy—a dead giveaway I've been crying.

"Where the hell are you?" Finn asks.

"I'm at Ferndale."

"What's that music? Are you having a party over there?"

"It's my roommates," I say. "They like to listen to it loud."

The beat drops out so all you hear is the rapper's voice saying, "These hoes is creeping on meeeee, peeping on meeeee. They want this thug for a baby daddyyyy."

"Do I need to come get you?" Finn asks.

"No, Finn. I'm fine." I grab my blanket and move

across the room to the closet before sliding to the floor in hopes the added wall space will help muffle the noise.

"Seriously, just say the word, and I'll get you out," Finn says.

"Finn. No," I repeat, louder this time. "You can't do that. The investigation, remember?"

Finn gets quiet. "I just want you to be safe," he says finally.

"I am safe. Besides, Amy says you can't come here without permission and definitely not outside visiting hours."

"Amy can shove it up her—"

"If you do," I go on, cutting him off, "you'll mess up your chance of getting approved to let me live with you until my birthday."

His grumbled curses blend with the rapper's.

"Amy said seven to ten days for your application. It's already been three. That means less than a week and I'll be out of here."

"Less than a week," he repeats reluctantly.

"Did you talk to Shelly at the gym?" I ask. "About holding my job?"

"Yeah, you're good," he says. "Don't worry."

"Thanks."

We sit in silence for a moment.

I pick absently at a loose thread on the hem of the blanket then stop myself when I realize if I keep pulling on it, the whole thing will likely unravel.

"El?"

"Yeah?" I say.

"I miss you."

My throat nearly closes. I want to tell him I miss him too, but that would be too much right now even with the Xanax coating the worst of it. Instead, I say, "She's in trouble, Finn. I know it."

"We'll find her, El. You just have to get home first."

His tone is absolute. The fact that he says 'home' like that's where I'll be when I go live with him stings my eyes.

"Do you think they'll catch the thing I saw?"

"El, sometimes when people are really scared, their brain conjures images. Things that aren't there. In order to explain something they don't want to face."

My heart seizes then cracks in two. He thinks I'm as crazy as the rest of them do.

"I didn't imagine it," I say, but there's no real fire behind my words.

"Then no, I don't think they'll catch it," he says so quickly I'm not sure if I've heard him right.

"But you just said—"

"If that red-eyed monster exists and is capable of disappearing a person without a trace, do you really think human police are going to find it?"

I blink, taken aback by his response. He's obviously given this some thought already. "Probably not," I say. "Does this mean you believe me?"

"I support you, El. No matter what. And I just want you safe which means you need to be here. With me. Where I can protect you."

The words are so comforting, and my heart is so desperate for them that I shove aside my questions.

"I want that too, Finn. I miss you." My voice cracks, and tears pool in my eyes.

"I'm going to find out about visiting hours and try to come see you tomorrow, okay?"

"Okay."

I start to hang up, but Finn says my name again.

"Yeah?"

"By the time your birthday rolls around, things will be different. It'll be better. No matter what they say about that stupid application, in a few weeks, you'll be eighteen which means you'll be free to go. And you'll be here. With me. You won't be alone. You won't be afraid. You'll see, El. Things will be better."

"Okay," I whisper.

However, the moment we're off the phone, the loneliness crowds in again. The Xanax is wearing off, and the music is louder now. But worse than that, the sun is gone.

Darkness has set in hard outside my steel-fortified window. There's a draft seeping through the cracks that feels like it's laced with more than just the winter's lingering chill. Fingers. Tendrils of claws. Eyes. Something dark rides on the draft and sends chills shuddering through me.

I climb back into bed and burrow deeper into the blankets, shivering until my teeth chatter.

Someone bangs hard on my door, eliciting a short scream from my raw throat.

"What?" I ask.

"Dinner, bitch," a stranger calls from the other side.

I've skipped dinner three days running, and I don't intend to break my streak now.

Something cold and clingy reaches for me from the

window. When I look, there's nothing there. Not even a whisper of the screams I heard that night. But I can feel the presence just the same as if it's waiting for me outside.

Somehow, I sleep.

My dreams are dark and menacing, and when I wake a few hours later, my clothes are damp with a cold sweat, and the house is finally, blessedly quiet. Somehow, the lack of noise is worse.

Fear snakes up along my spine and tickles my neck. Something is looking for me. Something dark and capable of slipping in through impossible places. Something more powerful than the strange black ink I can still feel like a second skin over my heart.

I have to get out.

The moment the thought arises, I leap up.

I rifle through my bag for fresh clothes and change quickly, hyper-aware of the feeling that *something* is watching me do it. My shoes are next then a ball cap pulled low over my ears and forehead. At the last second, I toss my phone back onto the bed and grab the bottle of Xanax before easing open the door and slipping out.

The hall is dark but empty.

I take the stairs as quietly as possible, my breaths shallow, my palm sweaty where it grips the bannister. At the bottom, moonlight streams in through a skylight above me, and I pause. Nothing moves, and I strain to hear some sound or sign that my fears are warranted, that I'm not alone.

But the house is silent and still.

I keep moving, stopping at the front door. It's

HEATHER HILDENBRAND

secured with a deadbolt that's held fast by a combination lock. No way am I getting through that. Not without the combination or a pair of bolt cutters.

I remember the light that came out of my hand and, feeling stupid, place my hand over the cold metal. Nothing happens.

Frustrated, I double back toward the kitchen in search of another door and find one off the laundry room. It, too, is secured with a deadbolt. This one has a keypad rather than a combination lock.

My irritation spikes, and I slam my hand over the cold metal pad. There's a soft beep and the door is pulled open from the outside.

I let out a shriek and scramble back as a figure in a black hood rushes in and clamps a hand over my mouth.

"It's me. Okay? Calm down," Finn says. "You're safe. Please don't scream."

I relax and reach up to pry his hand away.

"What the hell are you doing here?" I hiss.

"You needed me," he says simply. His honey-brown eyes make it clear that, for him, it's as simple as that.

"How did you get the door open?"

"Come home with me," he says.

"Finn, I can't. If they find out you were even here, they'll deny your application."

"I don't give a shit about the application," he whispers. "And neither do you. Or were you going someplace besides my house just now?"

I sigh. "Fine. I was going to see you."

He grins. "Then come on."

He turns and tugs me through the back door.

The moment I step out into the foggy night, my pulse races. I force myself to take a slow breath like Aerina taught me.

"Is it darker than usual?" I ask as Finn shuts the door behind us with a soft click.

He glances upward, frowning. "New moon."

He peers up and down the street and starts down the sidewalk. A few cars roll by. Unfortunately, Ferndale House is set on one of the busier streets of the downtown area.

"Come on. We'll cut through the woods," Finn says. He grabs my hand and tugs me toward the tree line.

"What?" I plant my feet, refusing to follow him into anything darker than the glow of the dim street lights where we currently stand. "Why would we do that? Didn't you drive here?"

"No, it would have drawn too much attention."

"You're telling me you walked all the way here from your house?"

He frowns, and there's something off about his expression.

"Finn. What's going on? Why are you really here?"

He blinks, and the frown vanishes. His hand tightens around mine impatiently. "You needed me, El. I told you. I'm not leaving you here any longer. Just trust me, okay?"

He nods at the woods. Between here and there, a blanket of fog lays over the ground, and my mind conjures all sorts of monsters I might meet if we walk through it.

I hesitate, but it's a losing battle, and we both

know it. Without Finn's car, cutting through the woods is the fastest escape. I glance back at the house behind me, my gaze traveling upward to the barred window that is my bedroom now.

In the room beside mine, a light suddenly flicks on, and panic spears through me. The thought of returning to it is just as bad as the prospect of the woods at night. At least in the woods, I'll be with Finn.

"El." Finn tugs again, harder this time. "We have to go."

I give in and hurry with him. A chill works its way underneath my coat, and I bite my lip against the urge to argue.

"Do you want me to carry you?" he asks when we reach the edge of the trees.

The fog curls against my back, tickling my senses until I'm positive something is watching us, but I shake my head. I refuse to turn and look.

"No."

"Stay close."

Behind us, the back door to Ferndale House opens and someone curses.

"Brand, what the fuck?" a person yells a second later.

I roll my eyes. They don't even get my name right.

"Get your ass back here!" The voice travels through the fog.

With Finn's hand over mine, we slip into the trees. The yelling and cursing coming from Ferndale House slowly fades.

Overhead, branches rustle with a wind that lifts the ends of my hair. My steps sound loud against the silence. Finn's are barely discernable. I stare at his feet for a moment, concentrating on his methods and trying to copy them.

The feeling of being watched never leaves me, but I don't turn to look.

Nothing, I tell myself. *There's nothing there.*

Finn suddenly stiffens beside me, and I immediately halt.

"What is it?" I ask.

He looks down at me with an urgency I've never seen before and holds his finger against my mouth, silencing me.

I blink, listening. The wind is as soft and eerie as ever. The leaves shake tenuously from the branches overhead.

Somewhere nearby, a branch breaks.

"Shit," Finn mutters, shattering what little sense of safety I have left. It's not the word he's said but the way he's said it, and I know. I was right all along.

We're not alone.

The wind howls through the fog-laced branches, and I shiver. A second later, I realize it's not the wind making the sound that's haunted my nightmares for the past three nights. It's an army.

A flying army of red-eyed monsters with wings twice the length of their beastly bodies. And they're headed straight for us.

"El, listen to me. No matter what you see next, I want you to—"

One of the monsters, a flying horse with a rippling, black coat and giant onyx wings, dives through the canopy overhead. It's aimed straight for me. Its jaw is wide open, revealing sharpened teeth. The sound it emits from its throat is something between a howl and a scream.

Trapped in the memory of their last attack, I can't even lift my hands to cover my ears. I stand there, struck by the absolute certainty my life is about to end. The monster's lips pull back in a disgusting smile because it knows it too.

Something big and uncontrollable surges inside me. My skin warms, and . . . I'm dragged sideways and tossed hard. I freefall for a split second before colliding with a bed of old leaves. Rolling awkwardly, I lift my head to see the monster has crashed into a tree instead of me.

Overhead, more winged monsters begin to descend.

Before they get close, a growl sounds from nearby. They change direction, diving for the ground not too far away.

I look at the wolf standing guard over me, its massive front paws positioned by my legs. I recognize the sandy fur. It's my savior from the other night. The wolf I hurt with my weird light-bolt trick.

I feel relief.

He's not like them. He's not here to kill me.

The escalation in the screaming draws my attention to the monsters. They are wrapped up in some sort of ground fight against something. My wolf shifts closer, blotting out my view, and I feel the same brush of awareness in my head that first sent me into a panic the other night.

We should run now while they're distracted.

The voice is low and urgent, and I can't help but wonder if it would sound so deep if he could speak out loud or if it's some weird thing my own head is doing to it.

The wolf glances at me, and I realize he's probably waiting for an answer.

"Right. Escape." Escape sounds good.

I start to get up, and a monster breaks from the pack in favor of attacking me. The sandy wolf leaps in front of me and launches itself at the monster.

Scrambling to my feet, I stare, wide-eyed, as the pair attack each other. This close, I see the monster really is built like a horse—a very tall, very evil, very rabid-looking horse. But despite the pointed teeth and menacing howl, the wolf isn't deterred. He's faster. That much is clear as he races in and out of the monster's reach, nipping and clawing until he's drawn blood from several places along the monster-horse's flank.

The monster-horse unfurls a wing, and something shiny glints against the darkness. The edge of the wing slices outward and catches the wolf's ear. The wolf yelps and falls back, crimson liquid leaking from its open wound. But it only seems to fuel the wolf's determination more.

I quickly scan for Finn, but he's nowhere in sight.

The cluster of monster-horses breaks apart suddenly, and three of the five creatures spread their wings and take to the sky.

I duck behind a tree and press my body against it.

The remaining two spin and scan the area as if looking for something—*me*, the fear in my head whispers. When they don't see me, they settle on the sandy wolf and begin to close in on him.

Fear squeezes my throat, and I try to think of some way to warn him.

"Elidi." Finn's voice is a whisper from behind me.

I whirl.

Shirtless and breathless, Finn steps from a cluster of bushes. His chest and arms are covered in scratches, and a cut on his forehead is bleeding down his cheek.

"Are you okay?" I rush to him.

"I'm fine. We have to run." He grabs my hand and yanks hard in the direction we've just come from.

"What?" I plant my feet, yanking against him. "But the wolf."

"Leave him," Finn says, the venom in his tone confusing me.

"But he saved me," I say. "Twice."

Finn's eyes narrow.

"What do you mean twice?"

"The night of the attack, he saved me. He fought these monsters off for me."

Finn's expression darkens.

"You should have told me about him."

"Why? I told you about the monsters, and you didn't believe me." Finn doesn't argue it. "Do you know what they want?" I ask.

"Dammit, El. I don't have time to explain this right now. Just come with me. I have to get you out of here."

"Explain what?" I yank hard against Finn's grip, wrenching my arm out of his hold.

Behind me, the wolf yelps again, and I whirl, worried.

I catch sight of him darting out of the way just as a pair of teeth snap closed on the empty air where he had stood. The monster lunges, but the wolf sidesteps again, this time raising its head long enough to meet my eyes.

For a fleeting moment, recognition washes over me again. Just like three nights ago, it's undeniable. Like a punch in the gut. Real and raw and not something I can ignore. And I damn sure can't let him die in my place.

I whirl on Finn.

"You go," I tell him. "I'm staying to help."

Finn's eyes go wide. "El, you can't fight them. You're not ready, and you're not immortal. You'll die."

I blink at his odd words. Then shake my head.

"I won't let him get killed for me."

Finn's expression says he's torn between staying with me and just carrying me off. I brace myself for the latter.

But he just looks upward and mutters, "This is insane. The Silenci aren't supposed to attack your kind."

The fact that he's keeping secrets registers like a physical blow.

"Goodbye, Finn," I say. Then I turn on my heel and march away from him, straight for the fight raging ahead.

My eyes catch on a fallen branch. I scoop it up, gripping it tightly in both hands as I approach the closest monster from behind.

The sandy wolf spins, nipping at one monster's throat before turning to do the same to the others, barely holding the group at bay. I inch closer.

Only a few feet away, I raise the branch over my head. The branch is heavy as I grip it tightly, preparing to strike the flank of the closest monster-horse.

I launch myself forward and shove the branch into the monster's flesh—hard. Its howl falters as the branch sinks through the first layer of flesh. Blood sprays from the wound, and I gasp at the sight and feel of it as it hits my cheeks and nose.

My stomach rolls.

The monster screams and lurches sideways. I grip the branch tighter and am yanked clear off my feet as the beast goes berserk. For the second time tonight, I'm completely airborne. This time, however, my eyes are wide open, and I'm fully aware of a trajectory I can't stop or alter.

I land on the back of the monster and have no choice but to hold tight as it pushes off from the ground and beats its wings trying to gain access to the open sky. I cling tightly with both hands as I watch the ground get farther and farther away from me.

Eerie screams rise up around me, and the beast beneath me stops fighting the fact that I'm now its passenger and adjusts in order to balance my weight.

Goddess, get your ass back down here now!

I wince at the volume of that order.

"Elidi!" Finn yells from below.

I look down and see him hovering below me, arms outstretched. He's also completely naked.

The horse veers sharply right to avoid a branch, and something sharp jabs my thigh. I gasp then remember the Xanax bottle. With one hand clinging to the horse, I slide the bottle out with the other then shove the cap off with my thumb. A few pills spill out and fall to the ground, but I fling the rest of them down and around, managing to land a few inside the horse's open mouth.

It bucks and screams, clearly pissed.

My balance teeters.

Pitching away from the murderous steed, I scream and let myself freefall to Finn's waiting arms below.

The force with which I hit Finn's arms is enough to bruise my back and legs. I blink up at him, stunned. Above him, I see the monster doubling back for us.

"We have to go," I say, scrambling out of Finn's arms.

"Isn't that what I've been saying?" Finn asks, crossing his arms and drawing my attention to the full display of his body.

I flush. He's even more impressive than I'd imagined. Not that I'd imagined Finn naked. He's my friend. But a girl can appreciate a fine-ass manly form when she sees—

"El!" Finn's sharp voice brings me back. "What are you waiting for?"

I look for the sandy wolf and spot him beside a tree. Even though he's a furry-faced wolf, he manages to look pissed.

What was that? he demands.

That was me saving your ass, I think, hoping he meant the branch stunt, not my ogling of Finn.

"Run," I call, and the wolf doesn't wait around for me to say it twice.

He turns and leaps into the woods, and I follow. Finn runs beside me.

Up ahead, the wolf disappears for a moment, and I slow, wondering if he's changed his mind about helping us. But then he reappears, standing on a fallen log as if to signal the way. When I get close, he turns and takes off again.

For the next few minutes, the wolf leads us, and I do my best to follow. Finn is at my heels.

Behind us, the screeching continues, letting me know we're being pursued and we're not far enough to have lost them yet. Hooves crash through the leaves in our wake, urging me faster.

Suddenly, a branch breaks in the treetops behind me. I whirl in time to see one of the horses crashing through branches as it plummets to the ground. It lands with a thud then goes still.

"What the hell?" Finn breathes.

"Finally."

He cuts me a look.

"What did you do?"

"Xanaxed him," I say.

Finn opens his mouth, but screeching from above drowns him out. I turn to run again because the sleeping beast's friends are obviously unhappy about their friend being drugged.

"El, we need to go back the other way," Finn says.

"I think this wolf will take us somewhere safe."

"That wolf is a half-breed and an idiot if he thinks he's going to protect you. You belong with me. I can help you harness what's inside you better than he can."

"Wait." I stop short and whirl on him. "You know what I can do?"

The howling changes direction and melds with the

sound of wings beating above us, but the monsters aren't visible. I can only hope that means we've lost them for the moment. Maybe the fog isn't such a bad thing after all.

"How the hell do you know anything about that wolf?" I point at where the sandy wolf has stopped to wait. "Or what's inside me? What are you not telling me, Finn? Why are you lying?"

"El," he begins, and I can hear it in his voice—the denial. The excuses. More lies.

"I'm not going anywhere with you until you tell me the truth." I step out of his reach just in case.

Finn's gaze flicks over my shoulder to the wolf, and his expression hardens.

"I can't tell you," Finn says, defeat lacing his words. "Not all of it, not yet. But I can keep you safe, and I can tell you that you shouldn't go with that asshole. Not ever."

My heart hurts to realize Finn might be on a different side than mine.

"You mean like you've kept me safe already?"

"Not fair, El," he says.

"I'm not going back with you, Finn. So you can come with us or stay behind. It's up to you."

Finn studies me for a long moment before he nods slowly, "Fine."

Finn takes a step away from me.

"I'll hold them off," he says, his light brown eyes sad now. "So you can get away."

I wither inside as I realize what he's chosen. The prospect of watching him walk away from me is the most painful thing I can imagine.

Rather than watch it play out, I spin on my heel.

"Fine," I call over my shoulder, closing the distance between me and the sandy wolf who waits just ahead.

His large eyes aren't on me, though. They're on Finn. When I finally reach the wolf, his gaze flicks to mine and holds there.

"We have to go," I tell him. "Do you know somewhere safe?" Overhead, I can hear the flap of approaching wings, and my pulse races.

Yes.

"Take me there," I tell him, and he blinks then turns to lead us away again.

I allow myself a single glance back, but Finn is already gone.

CHAPTER FOUR

THE woods go on and on. For hours, I do my best to follow my new friend, but my energy flags, and exhaustion creeps in. The sky lightens around us with the coming day. But for once, daylight isn't welcome. It's too exposing.

By the time the wolf finally stops to rest, I'm swaying on my feet.

"Are we almost there?" I ask, collapsing to the ground.

We're still being tracked, he says in my mind.

"You can still hear them?" I strain to hear the sounds of wings or hooves. But there's nothing beyond the birds and crickets.

Come on.

He turns to continue, and I struggle to my feet. My legs ache, and my knees threaten to buckle. I try to follow, but my body has other ideas. With a stumble, I find myself on all fours, just like my wolf. Our eyes meet, and I feel myself going under, the pull irresistible like a daymare.

"Just twenty minutes," I mumble.

Giving into the exhaustion feels good.

Nausea wakes me. The continuous rolling-bounce sensation makes it worse.

"Ugh," I groan. I brace my hands under me to lift myself upright and feel fur.

"What the hell?"

Groggy, I lift my head and wince at the sharp, lancing pain driving down the center of my skull. The pain doesn't distract me from what is happening, though.

I'm riding on the back of a wolf. Strapped to his back, effectively seat belted to him. And thank God since he is currently sprinting through a freezing forest at top speed.

There was no time to rest, he says as if that's reason enough to have snatched me away like this.

"You have got to be kidding me," I grumble. He doesn't answer, and I do my best to settle more comfortably or minimize the jostling—not that it works.

"How are you able to talk in my head?" I ask.

I'm a protector.

Something about the way he says it makes it sound like a title. "And as a protector, you can communicate telepathically," I say.

Let's just say it's one of my many talents.

His tone is smug, and I scowl. Fantastic. A snarky telepathic wolf. Just my luck.

Actually, I'm a divinely chosen protector who just saved your ass from a legion of The Silenci.

"What are Silenci?" I ask.

He hesitates. *You don't want to know.*

Further questioning is cut short by the sound of wind stirring the leaves around us. It's not a slight breeze but a gust that shakes the branches overhead until they're creaking loudly. The leaves shiver before being ripped away to rain down on our heads. The ground beneath us shakes hard enough to raise goose bumps on my arms and legs.

Shit. Hang on.

His muscles bunch and push harder as he takes off at a full-out sprint. I duck my head, wrapping my arms low for a better grip then burying my fingers in the thick fur around his throat. Branches catch on my hair, yanking the ends until sharp breaths hiss from my teeth. Behind us, the caw of birds as they're ousted from their nests becomes a battle cry. Wings beat the air, stirring the treetops as a flock of something pursues us overhead.

My pulse races.

Silenci.

Is that what the horse-monsters are called?

Can you swim?

The question rings out in my head, jarring me. "What?"

Never mind, hold your breath.

My mouth is wide open when the wolf plunges over the edge of a cliff I never saw coming. For a split second, we hang in mid-air—beast and human held together in a sort of magical suspension.

And then we fall.

The force of gravity steals my breath, and a scream gets caught in my throat, swallowed up by the way my stomach leaps into my chest.

My mother's face swims in front of me, reassuring me as if this isn't my last moment alive. As if the giant wolf with an attitude didn't just kill us both to save me from a flock of flying horse-demons.

They aren't demons.

It's the last thing I hear before we crash against the surface of the river below.

The impact stings like nothing I've ever experienced, and I know that if we make it out of this, my body will be bruised in places I never thought possible. My head pounds, and an instant later, water fills my throat before I remember not to inhale.

It tastes like my nightmares.

My arms flail, and my feet kick, but it does me zero good thanks to the leather strap still attaching me to my crazy-ass savior.

Not that way.

His voice is urgent and tense in my head, and it takes me a moment to realize he's kicking his legs in an attempt to swim *away* from the surface.

The water burns my eyes, and the darkness makes it impossible to see anything down here, but suicide-wolf swims hard like he knows where he's going and he can't wait to get there.

My lungs scream, and I know I have only seconds left before my body's reflexes take over.

Drowning.

Aerina insisted the dreams were a metaphor. I'd begun to believe her. Apparently, the universe has a much sicker sense of humor when it comes to me because I am, in this moment, living out my waking nightmare. And the dozens of "practice" drills I've experienced until now do me no good.

I'm still drowning.

My body strains with the need to breathe, and still the wolf continues to propel us through the murky water.

Asshole, I think.

The wolf snarls in my mind and continues to swim like he's done this a million times.

Finally, when I can't hold on a second longer, we break the surface, and I gasp for air, choking on the dregs of brackish water that tastes slimy on my tongue. The wolf's massive paws tread underneath us until they bump the sandy bottom, and then he walks us up and out of the water onto shore.

The cliff's edge rises high behind us, but all I can think is that I'm alive. I've survived the nightmare. That has to count for something.

Not only that, the world is quiet around us, empty of wings or caws or anything else that threatens to shatter my newfound sense of survival.

The wolf manages a few more steps before he lowers himself to the sand. His entire body heaves with labored breaths, and I fumble for the leather strap, attempting to free myself from his back so he can breathe easier.

But my fingers are cold and numb and not nearly nimble enough, and the leather strap wins out. Giving up, I huff then collapse onto his back, my heart still thundering and my own breaths still ragged. I press against him in a kind of hug, grateful he's saved us.

Shock or maybe awareness settles in, and I begin to shake.

This has officially been the worst week of my entire life. Aerina and now Finn. I'm alone. And, I realize as I stare at our surroundings, in an unfamiliar place.

During our trek, I had recognized we were still somewhere inside the Olympic forest. But the trees are different now. None of them are indigenous to Washington or maybe even the west coast. I crane my neck to look up at the cliff and realize it's made up of dark clay that I've only ever seen in photos of exotic places.

Where the hell has the wolf taken me?

I bolt upright, grasping fistfuls of fur.

"Did you kidnap me?"

The wolf doesn't reply, and I open my mouth to demand answers. Before I can manage a single word, the air between us warms, heating my drenched skin. The wolf shakes, but it isn't a shiver. More like a seizure.

My eyes go wide, and I try to scramble off of him. The strap stops me so I only manage a sort of shimmy that ends with me hugging his belly instead of his back.

"What—"

The very air around me crackles with an electric sort of energy and then *pop!*

The wolf is gone.

No more fur. No more paws and snout.

In its place is a very human, very male, very muscular and hard body. Broad shoulders. Large biceps. Chiseled chest. Washboard abs. And I'm sprawled all over it.

I blink down into dark eyes that are so brown they're nearly black. They stare up at me with an intensity I feel all the way to my suddenly very liquid bones. His jawline is sharp and angled into a neck corded with muscle. His dark hair is still damp and tousled, and one side of his face is coated in sand. He's warm and utterly dangerous and there's an edge in his intrigued expression that suggests it would be a bad idea to make a wrong move just now.

Except I don't know any right ones.

"How did you do that?" I ask, one of the bazillion questions spinning through my mind.

His gaze drops to my lips, and my mouth goes dry.

My heartbeat drowns out the sound of my own voice, and heat creeps up my throat and into my cheeks. His body is perfectly molded to mine, and the proof of how much he likes it presses into my thigh. It takes everything in me not to lower my mouth to his. Or to reach out and feel for his massive "interest" with my hands. But I don't.

Mostly because that's not me and also because this dude was just a wolf, and I'm pretty sure having sex with animals is illegal.

"Fuck me," I mutter when I remember how he'd been in my head up until a moment ago. Now that deep baritone makes sense.

His eyebrows go up, and his mouth twitches. "Now?"

"What?" I blink then freeze as I realize what I've said. "No. Shit."

I press my palms into his chest and try to climb off of him, but the leather strap holds me in place. Or more precisely, holds our groins in place. The effect is even more pressure between his "interest" and mine.

"Shit," I say again.

Wolf-man grins. "Here." He reaches down and, without taking his eyes off mine, releases the leather strap holding us together.

I immediately roll off of him with an "oomph" as my already-sore body hits the sand with a painful thud.

"Better?" he asks.

I roll over and raise my head to look up at him, unsure whether to thank him or scream or just turn around and wade right back into the river we've just come out of.

"Who are you?" I ask finally, too exhausted to do any of those things.

Wolf-man sits up, studying me intently for a long moment. So long that I wonder if he intends on answering me or if he prefers communicating telepathically over verbally.

Finally, he exhales, and something in his dark gaze settles as if he's made a hard decision and intends to live with it.

"My name is Kol," he says quietly. "I'm your chosen protector."

"Protector from what? Like a bodyguard? Why do I need that, and how did you just change?"

"All gods have protectors," he says. "And your case is especially urgent, considering there's actually someone trying to kill you. Lots of someones. Namely, The Silenci."

"Whoa." I hold up a hand to try and halt the crazy train that's currently speeding out of his mouth. "Did you just say gods?"

He frowns like he can't quite believe I'm confused

over the whole thing. Like I'm the one having a hard time grasping reality.

"You're a goddess, Elidi. The Goddess of Light to be specific. Or you will be. Right now, the proper term is goddess ascending."

"Goddess." I swallow hard, my eyes blurring as the world tilts and spins.

"Ascending," he adds, frowning now. Or at least, I think he's frowning. It's hard to tell through the blurred haze.

"Didn't your boyfriend explain?" he asks with a scowl.

I stare blankly back at Wolf-man as I try to make sense of what he's just said. However, all the staring does is make me forget what we were talking about in the first place. His eyes are like secrets or mysteries waiting to be unraveled, and I desperately want to be the one to unravel them.

"Say something," Kol says.

I blink. "Am I dead?" I blurt.

"No." He shakes his head, and I'm mesmerized by the tiny droplets of water that fling from the ends of his messy hair. "Thanks to me, you're very much alive. Although, our tandem diving skills need some serious work."

I try not to think about the almost-drowning that was literally a dream come true for me. Or nightmare. Whatever.

"You just kidnapped me and are complaining about my diving skills?"

"Carried you," he corrects. "For your safety. Alive, remember?"

"And Aerina?" My chin wobbles.

Kol's expression darkens. "I'm sorry I didn't get there in time," he says quietly.

"In time for what? What are those things? The screaming was. . ." I didn't even know how to describe it.

"The Silenci," he says grimly.

"The Silenci," I repeat.

He shakes his head and says, "It doesn't make any sense. The Silenci don't attack gods. Not to mention, they're relegated to the veil. How did they get across?"

I stare back at him, waiting for something he's just said to make any sort of logical sense. When it doesn't, I wave a hand to catch his attention.

"Uh, hello. Sane person here. Can we try to contain the explanations to things that are real?"

"What?" He sighs. "The Silenci are real, and they shouldn't have been able to do any harm to your aunt. They were created to protect gods, not hunt them. And they're relegated to the other side of the veil, specifically to guard the Gate of the Dead. I've never seen them hunt gods."

"Your aunt isn't dead," he says, confirming what I've believed since the moment she disappeared. The relief is so sweet that, for a moment, I don't trust it.

"How do you know? Are you sure?"

"If they were going to kill her, they'd have ripped her apart," he says quietly. "Besides, I saw her leave through a portal, which means they took her. What I don't understand is why."

"Okay, this is ridiculous." I scramble to my feet, which isn't easy thanks to the sand and my stringy wet hair making me top-heavy and waterlogged. I wobble. Only a little, but it's enough to make Wolf-man jump up and extend his arms almost like he's spotting my floor routine or something.

I glare at him, which is mostly me taking out my frustration at my inability to storm off properly. "You're insane."

"You really don't believe any of this is real?" His tone is more challenging than anything else, and it pisses me off for several reasons.

"You're talking about horse-demons and veils and gods."

"I'm not lying, Elidi."

"What about you? Where did you come from? Why are you here?"

He goes still, and a shudder goes through me at the way his gaze sharpens on mine then heats. It's not threatening or dangerous—not physically. But it's scarier than The Silenci because I know whatever he's about to say is going to change things.

"I know you because I've dreamt of you," he says quietly.

"What kind of dreams?" I ask, my voice lilting at the direction of my thoughts.

His lips twitch knowingly, and there's a different sort of gleam in his eyes. He steps closer, reaching out to tuck a strand of my tangled hair behind my ear.

"Not that kind," he says with a chuckle. "Sorry to disappoint."

"You're hardly disappointing me," I shoot back, and he smirks.

"Good to know."

My eyes widen. "That's not what I—ugh. Stop distracting me. Answer the questions."

His smile dims, but the sparkle in his dark eyes remains. I get caught in the contrast of his gaze. Dark shadows swirl like secret pools, but when he looks at me with that half-smile, there's a lightness there. A single spark. Like a firework or a bolt of lightning—

"Hey, spitfire. You still with me?"

I blink, doing my best to shove aside all the tingly thoughts and paste on a scowl. For good measure, I cross my arms. "I don't have to tell you anything. You're the one who kidnapped me."

He groans. "We've been over this. I saved you. Look around." He gestures to the woods around us with a sweep of his muscled arm. "There are no Silenci here. We're inside the wall, and you're safe." He steps closer. "You're welcome."

I look away, desperate to not succumb to the crazy attraction I feel for him.

"I don't see any walls. We're outside, genius."

He rubs his wet hair with his hand. "I guess gorgeous and agreeable was too much to ask." He casts a look to the sky like he's talking to someone. "Is this punishment then?"

I glare at him, but when he looks back at me, his mouth is tilted in amusement.

"Look, I dreamt of you because I'm meant to protect you. I can't prove that, and you have nothing but my word and my track record. If I hadn't been there, The Silenci would have finished you off. That much I know for sure."

"Why do you think that?" I ask, intrigued enough

to let the comment about me being punishment slide—for now.

"Because of this." He hands me a rock, and my eyes widen at the familiar blood stains coating the top and sides.

"This was at my house," I say in shock. "It opened and . . . something came out. You . . . pushed me aside."

He nods. "A curse," he explains quietly. "Whoever sent it meant to kill you. I think Aerina was trying to take your place, and that's why she sent herself through that portal."

"But it hit me," I say, remembering the black inky coating over my heart. I run a hand absently over it at the memory.

"Not all of it." He rubs a dark spot on his chest. "I think I managed to soak up enough to keep it from really doing any damage to you."

I reach out and run my finger over the spot. A pulse of something courses from him to me, and I jerk away my hand.

"What was that?" I demand.

He looks just as shocked as me for once. "No idea. Curses are unpredictable." He shakes his head then steps back.

"What the hell," I whisper, stunned.

Wolf-man shakes his head again. "I don't think Hell has anything to do with this."

I snort. "You say that like you know the residents personally."

He shrugs. "I've only had direct dealings with the lower demons, but curses like this one aren't their style."

My jaw falls open. "What. The. Fuckery."

He cocks his head. "You really don't know what you are, do you?"

"I know I'm being held against my will," I say because it's clear to me that Kol has lost his marbles, and I've officially over-stayed my welcome inside his twisted little reality.

"Elidi, listen to me," he says, clearly on edge. "I don't know why no one told you the truth. Maybe it was to protect you. But we're past that now, and you need to know."

"Need to know what?" My heart bangs loudly against my ribs.

"You're not human, Elidi. Not entirely. And neither am I."

"What are you exactly?" I ask.

"I'm a wolf shifter. A guardian and protector of the gods created by Odin during the Great War. I'm here to protect you."

My mouth goes dry.

"This can't be real," I breathe.

My eyes fill with tears, and it pisses me off because crying seems like the least helpful thing my body can do for me now.

"You saw me shift from a wolf to this," he says, gesturing to his body, which doesn't help since the only thing covering him is a scrap of shorts that seems to have just barely made the transition with him from animal to human.

Not human.

He just said neither of us were human.

"You saw it with your own eyes," he continues. "I

was a wolf, and now I'm a man. Hard to deny it when you witnessed it firsthand."

"Hard, yes. Impossible, no," I say, but all the while, my brain is showing me images of things that I can't quite blow off as a product of a head injury. The glowing eyes. The Silenci's scream breaking a window. Aerina's reaction is the only thing I can't accept. The way she went to meet the danger. Like she'd already accepted the idea of giving her life. For me.

"Elidi," he says softly. And then in my head, *Elidi*.

"Fine, Wolf-man. Have it your way. You're not human."

"We're not human," he corrects.

I glare. "But cursed or not, we have to go back."

"The Silenci are out there waiting. We can't just go back."

"Aerina is the only family I have left," I say. "I have to find her."

He shakes his head. "I get that. I do. But it's too dangerous. The Silenci are probably still waiting on the other side of the wall, and I can't protect you against them all, spitfire. I'm good, but I'm not that good."

"Then you can stay here."

He barks out a laugh.

"Not happening," he says. "Like it or not, I'm in this."

"Well, feel free to take yourself out of it. I can do this on my own."

I take a step toward the water, but he grabs my wrist, spinning me around to face him. Heat brands me where his fingers touch my skin, and it's all I can do not to shiver and throw myself against him. The dark patch on his chest draws me, and I have to curl my fingers against the urge to touch it again. To touch him. And not just there but everywhere.

It's the shock. Has to be.

"The dreams and visions are binding for a protector, and mine have all been filled with you for months now. I can't leave, spitfire. I won't."

"What about me? Don't I get a choice?" I ask.

"I dream of drowning with you," he says softly, and I suck in a sharp breath.

My gaze searches his. There's more to it. Things he's not telling me. I can see it written in his fervent expression. But the drowning. The nightmares—I can't deny those.

"I don't trust you," I say.

It's a lie. Whatever I saw in him when our eyes locked during that lightning bolt, although crazy, left me with no doubt about one thing: I can trust Kol with my life.

I'm just not sure what kind of life that is anymore.

CHAPTER FIVE

KOL finally begins to look weary, and I can't help but be impressed by his stamina, considering it took this long.

"We need sleep. But first, I'll feed you," Kol says in a voice that brooks no argument.

"Fine," I say sweetly. "I'll take two double cheeseburgers and a vanilla shake."

Something zips across the beach to our left and catches his attention. He smirks, but whatever it is moves way too fast for me to see.

"How about a nice, warm rabbit stew instead?" he asks.

"Rabbit? You know what? I just remembered. I'm a vegetarian."

"Since when?"

"Since now." I wrinkle my nose.

"You have to eat, Elidi."

"If I wanted a pet dog to hunt my dinner, I would have gotten a Beagle or something manageable."

One minute, Kol's standing out of reach, and the

next, he's gripping my hips and has me backed against a tree. His scent, a heady musk that is all forest and wood chips, fills my nose. He's every inch brute force and raw power and staring at me so hard that I don't dare move.

"I'm not a dog, Elidi. I'm a wolf divinely created for the sole purpose of death and destruction to anyone who threatens my chosen. And I'm not your pet, although petting can be arranged." His eyes glitter with anticipation. "We'll think of it as a perk if you like."

My mouth goes dry, and my stomach tightens, sending a signal of distress straight to my heated center. Maybe distress isn't the right word. Maybe it's lust. Hard to tell without oxygen flowing to my brain.

Kol's hand trails my now-flushed cheek.

"Is this what you want?" he asks. *To pet me?*

The last few words echo inside my head, and the sound of that voice cutting through all my fantasies is enough to undo me.

"I want. . ."

As if sensing my weakening resolve, Kol lifts his other hand from the tree and places it over my heart. His palm pulses with a rhythm that perfectly matches my own heartbeat.

"Feel that?" he whispers.

I nod.

"We match. You are my chosen."

My skin tingles, and my nipples tighten which isn't something I can hide thanks to my wet shirt and then sports bra plastered against my chest.

Kol's eyelids droop, and he looks me over with a hungry expression. His mouth inches closer to mine.

A sudden pop behind the tree breaks me from his seductive spell.

Kol's eyes go wide, and he straightens away from me. His gaze flicks to something over my shoulder, and he lets out a heavy, irritated breath.

"Well, well, what am I walking into?" a smooth male voice says.

I guiltily slide away from Kol and look around the tree. In a glance, I note the stranger's mop of sandy-brown hair and definition underneath the dress shirt and slacks he's wearing. He's handsome in a boyish sort of way, but his eyes say there's nothing boyish or young about him.

"Hi, Grim," Kol says.

Grim grunts a reply then fastens his sharp gaze on me. There's something in his sweeping study of me that leaves me wishing for more. A pull that tempts me to wander closer, to—

"Grim," Kol barks. "Cut it out."

"Just getting to know your new chosen." The stranger winks at me. "Hi, I'm Grim, Kol's better-looking god friend."

I frown at the casual way he's just said "god."

"I'm Elidi."

"Oh, I know exactly who you are, darling. And aren't you divine to look at."

"What do you want?" Kol demands warily.

"Before I tell you that, I feel it's prudent to remind you that your oath of protection refers to preserving the life of your chosen, not ruining her virtue."

My cheeks heat. "We weren't doing anything."

"You better have come here for something more

important than a sex talk, Grim, or so help me," Kol says.

The stranger smirks. "Just thought you'd like to know Vayda got wind of your little rescue and has requested your presence." His gaze flicks to me. "Immediately."

"Fuck." Kol runs a hand through his unruly hair, and it's the first hint of worry I've seen in him so far.

"Who's Vayda?" I ask.

"Our stepmother," Grim says.

I look back and forth between them. "Wait. You guys are brothers?"

Grim shrugs. "You could say that."

"Not by blood," Kol says. "Especially Vayda."

Grim rolls his eyes. "Don't tell her that," he warns.

Kol's expression of concern doesn't change.

"What's the big deal?" I ask. "Family drama sucks, but you just deal with it."

Grim laughs. "Trust me. This isn't your usual family drama. Vayda only summons you when you've done something really right or really, really wrong."

I look at Kol dubiously. "Let me guess. You did the second thing?"

He doesn't meet my gaze. "You could say that."

"Well, just tell her no," I say, still confused as to why two strapping men look so afraid of their stepmother's invitation to visit.

Both of them share a look.

"You don't tell Vayda no," Grim says quietly, and some of his bravado vanishes.

"We have to go," Kol says.

"We?" I repeat. "No way. I can't go with you to

meet your mother. I have to go home."

"You can't go home, Elidi," he argues.

"You don't get to tell me what to do." I cross my arms.

"Listen, not to interrupt your lover's quarrel, because it's kind of adorable, but I feel the need to inform you that the home you knew is gone. Coming with us is the only way you live through this."

"Gone? What do you mean gone?"

"I mean, I just came from there. It's how I picked up your trail to find you here. And it's gone. Burned." His voice gentles at my expression. "Here. I'll show you."

With a sweep of his arm, a picture forms out of thin air. It's my yard.

Across the grass, I recognize Aerina's Prius in the driveway and the porch steps. That's all that remains of the house. In its place is a pile of blackened timber and debris. Curling smokestacks rise lazily from the embers.

A tall figure stands at the edge of the yard. Familiar broad shoulders. A red gas can dangles from his fingers.

"Finn," I whisper.

"He can't hear you," Grim tells me quietly.

"Is this real?" I ask, dumbstruck while my mind struggles to put the pieces together.

"It's real," Grim confirms.

"How?" I ask.

"I'm the God of Secrets," Grim says. "I can't always divulge what I know without upsetting the balance." Kol grunts, and Grim adds, "Fine, not without a price.

But this one . . ." His gaze flicks to me and he says, "This one I can do for free."

I stare at Finn's somber expression as he watches the fire die. His cheeks are streaked black as if he ventured too close at one point. Or was close when he first ignited the flames.

My throat closes with my pain. How could Finn just destroy the last bit of home that I had left? Something doesn't feel right, and I realize Finn knows more than he ever let on.

Grim snaps his fingers, and the image disappears with a quiet pop.

I look up at Kol, angry and defeated.

"Let me help you," he says quietly. "Let me make you safe."

I'm going to say yes. We both know it.

"Trust me, Elidi. Protecting you is my entire reason for existence, and I intend to honor that calling for as long as I live. You are my life now."

"And if I refuse your protection?" I ask.

He shrugs. "I'll follow you anyway, and when danger threatens, I'll do everything I can to save you from it until you're strong enough to save yourself."

"Save myself?"

"You don't know what you're becoming, but I do. Come with me. Let me show you the truth about what you are. After that, if you want to leave, I won't stop you."

"All right," I say, sighing. "Take me to your stepmother."

He nods, and I take two steps toward the woods before his hand comes around my waist to spin me around.

"Where are you going?" he asks.

"To your house?"

He shakes his head. "Not that way."

"Back into the water?" I ask, hoping not.

"No, I mean not on foot. We'll never make it in time."

Kol backs up a step then shudders as the air pops and crackles, and the edges of his skin shimmers then begins to morph. I squint against the sudden brightness emanating from his chest. I blink, and Kol is a wolf again.

He fetches the leather strap from the sand before trotting over to where I stand.

"No way," I protest. "If you're going to force me to ride with you, fine. But I will not be tied down again."

Kol rolls his eyes and drops the leather strap.

"You did not just roll your eyes at me."

He noses my palm, swiping his tongue up the length of it.

"What the—" I shriek, and the wolf's massive shoulders shake with laughter.

Come on, spitfire. We don't want to be late. Admit it. You love riding me.

CHAPTER SIX

THE trees zip past at a dizzying rate that threatens to empty my stomach. I shut my eyes and focus on breathing. Riding on the back of a wolf who is also a man hot enough to melt the panties off a Playboy bunny is more nauseating than exciting.

Underneath me, the powerful muscles of my wolf-protector ripple with his effort. My exhaustion makes it hard to tell whether it's been an hour or only a few minutes.

Kol slows suddenly, and I force my eyes open, terrified that The Silenci have somehow caught up to us. Instead of the red-eyed monsters, two massive wooden gates loom ahead.

Kol trots forward, and the gates creak and moan as they swing slowly open. Below me, my wolf-protector shifts his weight impatiently. I try not to think about what has him in such a hurry.

The moment there's enough room to squeeze through, he surges forward, and I grab a handful of fur to keep from doing a somersault off the back end of my furry transport.

On the other side of the gate, there are more trees. Something moves into my periphery, and I look, half-afraid one of the towering sentinels has come to life. But the trees haven't moved.

Between their gnarled branches, a beast steals its way closer to the gate. Closer to us.

The creature's green gaze locks with mine. My heart pounds as the beast halts. Its intense emerald stare calls me closer almost as strongly as if it has spoken my name aloud. A demand. An order to obey.

When I don't give in, the wolf pulls its lips back and bares its teeth. Fury wells up, and I tighten my fists around the fur in my hands. With a snarl of my own, I bare my teeth right back.

The wolf blinks, obviously thrown off by my response.

Then Kol and I are sprinting again, leaving the green-eyed wolf at the already-closing gates.

BY the time Kol comes to a stop and I dismount, we're standing near the top of a mountain peak, and I'm battling what I'm sure is a near-death case of hypothermia. Spring breezes have given way to winter along the way.

The wind has blown snowdrifts up against the copse of trees we're huddled inside, offering a bit of protection from the icy gusts. But even so, my teeth won't stop chattering. And my body, while numb, is aching with a bone-chilling cold.

Kol shifts into his human form, complete with skimpy shorts, and wraps his bare arms around me. I want to ask how in the hell he's so hot, but I'm not sure it would come out in the right context.

"Wh-what's w-wrong?" I manage to ask between chattering teeth.

"Shit. I forgot you're still so human," he says in my ear.

He scoops me into his arms and presses my cold body firmly against his warm chest. "Don't fight me on this," he says the minute my futile attempts to protest begin. "It'll keep you warm until we can get you some clothes and a fire."

I open my mouth to reply, but all that comes out is a moan. Not the noise I want him hearing while I'm pressed against his half-naked body. So I shut my mouth and make a mental note to chew his ass out later.

Kol climbs up the peak, and I burrow in closer to escape the wind. As we crest the peak and descend the other side, I catch sight of a small village spread out below us.

From here, the houses look like fancy tents complete with chimneys. Most importantly, there's no snow around them. It's as if the weather is different there than it was just a dozen yards back.

Kol slows a bit but doesn't offer to put me down as we approach, and my gaze catches on the people moving between the tents. They aren't quite human. When we reach the first row of housing, I see a redheaded girl floating along, her feet never touching the ground. There's also a half-man, half-horse creature that carries a spear in one hand and a dead rabbit in the other.

"See?" Kol's voice is full of laughter as he nods at the rabbit. "Dinner."

"N-not hungr-ry," I chatter while my stomach growls in betrayal.

Kol chuckles.

We reach the second line of tents and veer toward the one at the end just as a howl rises, high and wistful, against the winter-gray sky. Kol's arms tense around me, and I know the howl means something important. But he just ducks inside the tent flap.

The climate completely changes as we pass through the fabric-covered doorway. No hint of winter remains, and the air is thick with heat and humidity.

A roaring fire blazes in a center hearth, and thick rugs cover every inch of the floor, sealing the edges of the canvas walls with a cozy layer of privacy I hadn't expected.

"Is this your house?" I ask, still shivering.

Kol nods then crosses to a large bed covered in blankets and deposits me gently underneath the covers.

The bed's soft and already warm. I immediately feel the pull of sleep despite my empty stomach.

"I'll be back," he says then starts for the door.

"Wait. Where are you going?"

"To find you some warmer clothes. And maybe talk my stepmother into letting you rest before she interrogates you."

"What?"

He sighs then sits on the bed beside me. He

reaches for the blankets, tucking them up to my chin.

"Don't worry about it, spitfire. She won't hurt you."

"Interrogation doesn't' sound like a good thing," I say, my words almost slurring with my need to sleep.

"Just rest, okay?"

My lids droop even as I shake my head.

"That's what I thought," he murmurs, and it's the last thing I hear before I'm sucked into oblivion.

SOMETHING booms, waking me in a panic before I realize the sound was only another dream. No more water. This time, there was smoke and flames. All of it black as coal. I blink at the sight of the tent's interior then sit up and frown down at my damp clothes. I'm sweating.

My gaze catches on the fire still burning steadily in the center hearth. The flames haven't died down during my apparent power nap.

The front door flap opens, and Kol steps inside. He's clothed now, and his hair's a little less ruffled, but otherwise, he looks the same—right down to his brooding stare.

"You're awake." Relief flashes over Kol's expression, gone before I can commit it to memory.

"You're dressed," I say since we're apparently stating the obvious.

He closes the distance between us and hands me the jug in his hand. "Here."

I take the jug and tip it back, chugging half of it

before coming up for air.

"Thanks," I tell him, handing it back.

"Finish it. You need to hydrate."

For some reason, the sensible words sound funny to me. I snicker, earning a weird look from my wolf-protector.

He sits down on the edge of the bed and raises a finger.

"Follow my finger," he says, moving it left to right in front of my face.

I do, frowning. After a couple of back-and-forths, he drops his hand and then produces a flashlight from his pocket. He clicks it on and shines it directly into my right eye.

"What the heck?" I jerk out of his reach, but he just huffs and then tries again.

"Just let me check you out," he says.

I stop avoiding and grin slowly, which earns me a scowl.

"I mean check out your vision," he corrects.

"My vision's fine," I say, batting him away. "Why would you think it's not?"

"I'm checking for a concussion. Or shock. You hit the water pretty hard earlier, and then the temperature plunge didn't help."

"So?"

"So, you're laughing inappropriately and not making a whole lot of sense."

"*You* think I'm a goddess, and *I'm* the one who doesn't make sense?"

Without waiting for an answer, I swing my legs off the bed. My feet hit the rug, and I'm pleased to find it's just as warm as the rest of the room.

"How do you heat a tent so well?"

He smirks. "What can I say, spitfire. I'm just that hot."

My belly shivers with the fact that he's right, though I'm not about to let him know that.

Pretending my toes aren't threatening to curl, I roll my eyes, and we both push to our feet at the same time. My stomach tightens as the scent of something delicious wafts over from the pot on the stove.

"Mm. What is that?" I move toward the smell.

My knees wobble, and I make it no more than two steps before they go out. Kol catches me and scoops me up into his arms, saving me from yet another face plant.

I blink dizzily.

Kol's head swims into view, and I blink, a little put off by the fact that he's blurry.

"What just happened?" I ask, sitting up thanks to the hand he's pressing against my back.

The room tilts a little, and I stare down at my thighs, hoping it'll pass soon so I can try whatever mystery dinner is cooking. Priorities are to eat then pass out again—in that order.

"You just collapsed." Kol sounds worried—which makes me worry. "How do you feel?"

"Dizzy," I admit.

He grabs my hands and helps me stand but the minute he lets go, I sway. Strong hands latch around my shoulders, catching me and holding me upright. When another wave of dizziness washes over me, I tilt my head back, suddenly feeling more liquidy than solid. "Whoa," I mutter.

Before I know what's happening, I'm scooped off my feet and placed gently back in bed. Covers are tucked around me, and by the time I focus on the figure blocking my view, Kol is looming over me with his broody face back on.

"You look angry. I didn't break something of yours when I fell, did I?"

"You're cold again," he says, ignoring my question. "Are you still dizzy?"

"No. I told you. I don't have a concussion."

He doesn't look convinced, but he doesn't argue either.

My brain goes fuzzy, and I close my eyes. Kol says something else, but I'm already too lost to sleep to hear it.

When I open my eyes again, the room is darker. The fire still crackles animatedly in the hearth, but the flames are shoving against the shadows crouching in the corners of the space. Kol is nowhere to be found, but I hear low voices murmuring from the other side of the chimney that cuts through the center of the room.

"...her mortal soul can't survive on this side of the barrier," a woman says.

"It's not like I had a choice." Kol's familiar timbre is unmistakable. So is the stress lacing his words. "It was this or The Silenci."

"You made the best choice at the time," the woman agrees. "But humans can't survive on this side of the veil. The universal laws are too different here. Their bodies and minds reject it."

"Ascending," Kol says.

"A goddess ascending is still mortal enough to reject the magic, Kol." The voice is chastising now.

"But her goddess side—"

"Is awake." The woman's voice is amused, and I scowl at how smoothly she's just ruined my eavesdropping.

A second later, Kol appears from behind the chimney. His dark eyes are full of enough concern to make me wonder exactly how long I've been out.

"What time is it?" I ask, struggling to sit up before I realize I didn't really know what time it was before I passed out.

"Nearly midnight," Kol says. "On Thursday."

"You were asleep almost fifteen hours," says the woman behind him.

My eyes land on her, and I feel awe. She is gorgeous. Ethereal. I can't stop staring at her shiny blonde hair and perfectly sculpted cheekbones. Her skin is flawless and creamy with rosy cheeks.

She steps around Kol and clasps my hand with a gentle squeeze, a real smile curving her full mouth.

"Elidi, I'm Vayda," she says. "It's a pleasure to meet you."

"*You're* Kol's stepmother?" I ask. The woman doesn't look a day over thirty. Maybe Kol's dad has a thing for younger women?

Vayda smiles. "I am mother to all of Odin's creations."

"Odin? As in Thor's dad?" I ask, confused.

Vayda laughs. "Yes, well, some of our stories have spilled over into the human world. As for the rest of us," she sweeps her arms out to include Kol and maybe even this whole mountain town. "We're a little less recognizable, though I assure you, we're just as real."

I frown as I realize this woman brings no more sanity to the table than Kol does. They all think they're gods. Or wolves. And they think I'm a god too. Maybe it's the dizziness or the exhaustion, but I can't quite find it in me to argue anymore.

"How are you feeling?" Kol asks.

"Better." I attempt to sit up, and Kol stops me.

"Whoa. Just rest," he says.

"I can't afford to rest," I say, frustrated and impatient. "If I was out for fifteen hours, that means I've lost an entire day."

"And you're going to lose more than that if you don't rest," Kol says, blocking my attempts to get up.

"What's wrong with me?" I ask, stifling a yawn. "And don't tell me it's stress or something. I heard you talking."

Vayda quirks a brow at that and looks at Kol.

He sighs. "Your body's rejecting the magic of this place," Kol says.

"What magic?"

"Don't tell me you didn't feel it," Kol says.

An awareness prickles at the edge of my senses. Something I've been ignoring since gasping for breath on the shore.

"When we emerged from the river, we were no longer on the earthly plane," he says. "And don't tell me that's crazy because I know you felt it."

"I felt like I was drowning," I say.

Kol just gives me a look and says, "Exactly."

My eyes widen. "Hold up. You think my lungs

bursting for oxygen as you insanely swam away from the shore equates to leaving the earthly plane?" My gaze swings to Vayda since I can't trust Kol anymore.

"Kol's right, Elidi. You crossed what we call the veil."

"The veil?"

"It's a kind of curtain that separates the human world from the god realms."

"I'm not on Earth anymore?"

"You're still on Earth," she assures me. "Just not on the same plane that you're familiar with. Think of this place as a second reality overlaid against the reality you already know."

"And where is this second reality in relation to Earth's geography?" I ask.

"We're high in the mountains of the Wenatchee National Park," she explains.

I sigh because hearing the name of a location I recognize somehow normalizes all of this in a way the supermodel-fur-queen and her too-young-stepson can't.

"Why did we come here if it's making me sick?" I ask.

"Kol brought you to Black Peak to escape The Silenci. Unfortunately, your mortal body can't equalize in a place where the laws are so different from the world you know."

"Laws like what? Is kidnapping not illegal here?"

Vayda's smile widens. "You're sassy. I like it. It'll serve you well on this journey."

"What journey?" I ask, not sure I like how she makes it sound. Like it's about more than a swim through a magical river and glamping with Kol.

"You're ascending, Elidi." Vayda folds her hands in front of her, and I notice how angelic the pose makes her look. "It's not easy. You'll need all your strength to survive it."

"What I need strength for is finding my aunt Aerina. I mean, I don't even know if she's alive," I add, desperation leaking in.

"Aerina isn't dead," Vayda tells me.

"How do you know?"

"If The Silenci wanted her dead, they would have killed her. Kol told me she went through a portal. I've already dispatched my best trackers to find her. If she's on the Celestial plane or in any of the three realms, we'll find her."

"Did you just say Celestial?"

Vayda smiles. "Yes. It's the third of the six realms: Heavenly, Ethereal, Celestial, Bailiwick, Earth, and Gehenna."

"Okay, look. Can we just stop this family crazy train right there? You're both insane. Realms? Really? And for the record, Aerina can't be a goddess. She cheats at Scrabble, and she always doubles back for a second sample at the food court."

Vayda's brows rise.

"Being a goddess isn't about being a good person," Kol says, grinning.

"Then what determines it?" I ask.

"It's a matter of bloodline," he says.

Vayda nods. "You're born this way, darling."

They both watch me carefully, and the full meaning behind her words finally sinks in. "Are you saying I was born a goddess?" Whoa. "That means. Uh, no. No way. You think my mother was a goddess?"

"Hemera, Goddess of Day, to be exact," Kol says.

I snort. "Okay, now I know you're crazy. My mom was the least goddess-like person I knew. She drank and cursed like a sailor. And don't even get me started on her addiction to Hallmark Christmas movies. Wait." I frown as his words finally sink in. "How do you know her name?"

Kol cuts Vayda a look. "I think she hit her head before I got her out," he says like it explains everything.

That was it.

"Okay, look. As nice as you've been, providing me with a place to collapse and all, I need to get back." I toss back the covers, but Kol doesn't budge from where he's blocking my dismount off his large expanse of a mattress.

"Elidi, you can't leave," he says.

"We're back to kidnapping then?" I glare back at him, refusing to be intimidated.

"Actually, leaving is exactly what you need to do," Vayda says, laying a hand on Kol's shoulder.

"Thanks," I tell her with a smile. "Hoes before bros, am I right?"

I wiggle my toes, forcing Kol to take a step back, then push to my feet. The moment my toes hit the rug, the room sways. I grab the mattress as an anchor, plastering a smile on my face for my audience. Kol watches me dubiously, and I don't miss the way he hovers close as if ready to catch me when I go down.

I don't tell him to stop because the way the room is spinning, I have zero doubt it'll be necessary in three...

two...

Kol snatches me out of the air before I can hit the rug.

"Ugh," I groan as he sets me back in bed.

Vayda says something I don't catch, but Kol shakes his head, his dark eyes blazing now. "We can't move her. Not like this," he says.

"You can't leave her here," she warns. "Her body will only continue deteriorating."

"Where are we supposed to go?" he demands.

"Kol." In an instant, her tone changes, and she snaps the word hard enough that I flinch.

Kol stiffens and then turns to face her. Between them, energy buzzes, and while Vayda's expression is neutral and calm, there's a frenetic sort of impatience rolling off of her now. Like she's only barely holding onto the leash of her own power.

I stare up at her with wide eyes.

"You saved her despite the fact that you don't have a divine order," she says quietly, and there's a hint of rage behind her words now. "Even so, you are my own, and I won't deny you the honor of your oath. But you can't stop what's begun. And you can't control this. Especially not now."

Kol stares back at her for a long moment. "You knew I'd have to go to her," he says quietly, and there's accusation in his hushed words.

"She's the safest option for you now," Vayda says in a clipped voice.

In the silence between them, power shudders then clashes before fading away. Finally, Kol blinks and nods slowly.

"I'll need to make arrangements."

"Let her rest while you prepare. I'll have the healer check on her. Give her something to refresh her for the journey."

Kol looks back at me, but I can tell from his glazed eyes he's not seeing me now. He's making plans for whatever trip he and Vayda are discussing.

Frustrated at my cluelessness, I tighten my fists around a handful of sheets.

"Hello? Still here. Did you forget about me while you were discussing my life without my input?"

Vayda's lips twitch. "Forgive us. We're moving quickly to prevent your condition from worsening."

"So, Kol is taking me home?" I ask.

Vayda hesitates. "Not exactly."

She shares a look with Kol. "Your home is gone. Remember?" he asks gently.

"Shit," I say suddenly as the memory returns. "Shit," I say again when I realize I said shit in front of a beautiful goddess.

Vayda doesn't call me out, though. She just waits, watching me like she expects me to do something other than sit here muttering curses.

"My aunt Aerina," I say. "You're sure she's not dead?"

"I'm almost positive," she says.

"How do you know?"

"Put simply? Aerina is the Goddess of the Morning. Without your mother here, losing Aerina would be . . . let's just say there'd be consequences for your reality. Noticeable changes."

"What kind of changes?" I ask.

"Let's just say, the fact that the sun came up this morning is a good sign."

I blink, completely dumbfounded at her words. Disbelief rises, but I shove it down. If I'm going to ask for Vayda's help finding Aerina, I have to play by her rules.

"How can I find her?" I ask. "How do I bring her home?"

Vayda hesitates. "You would have to travel through the veil, which isn't something your mortal body can handle."

"But you said I'm a goddess."

"Not yet, you're not. And until then, you're not capable of making that journey."

"Fine. Tell me what to do in order to become that strong," I say.

Vayda's gaze sharpens, and she gives me a once-over like she's still expecting me to shake the exhaustion clinging to my bones.

"There's only one way you can save her now," she says.

"Tell me."

"You have to ascend."

CHAPTER SEVEN

I have to ascend.

What does that even mean? Like climb a hill? My foggy brain can't seem to work her words into a sensible context, and Vayda doesn't even stick around to clarify. One minute she's perched on the edge of my bed like some sort of ethereal nursemaid, and the next she's pushing to her feet and snapping orders to Kol who's hurrying around the room, shoving things into a brown duffel like there's a fire drill.

It might have been infuriating or even disturbing if I wasn't so damned dizzy. And sleepy. Somewhere between Vayda's personality shift and Kol's brooding, I drift off again.

When I wake, the tent is darker than before, and the fire has been reduced to embers. My throat aches, and my body feels twice as heavy as normal, but I'm determined to move.

I peel the blankets back and then freeze at the sight of my own body or, more importantly, what's covering it. My yoga pants and sports bra are gone, replaced by thick socks, leggings and a cotton tunic. They're warm thanks to the durable fabric, and cozy too, but I can't help wondering who changed me: Kol or his mama.

Either possibility feels awkward as hell, so I decide not to wonder too hard and concentrate on swinging my legs over the edge of the bed.

No one rushes to stop me, which proves I'm finally truly alone, and after three tries, I manage to stand. My legs immediately wobble, but I managed to make it over to the water jug someone has set on the center counter. My stomach growls while I chug the contents.

After I finish, I carefully walk around looking for something to eat, but I can't find any food among the cabinets or stacked barrels. Apparently, Kol has packed up nearly everything that hasn't been nailed down. It makes me wonder exactly where he plans on taking me when we leave here. And for how long. Not that it matters.

Aerina is alive. And if I get my shit together and stop fainting long enough to "ascend," I can probably save her, because apparently, I'm a goddess too.

A pair of boots stand beside the entrance. I slide my feet inside and find that they're exactly my size.

I manage to leave the tent without blacking out, but my breath is short. However, the cold helps revive me enough that I can step away from the tent and look around.

Unlike at my arrival, there are no other people in sight. The moon has risen high over the hillside, illuminating the snow. Overhead, stars twinkle through the bared branches.

The other half-dozen tents I can see from where I

stand each have a steady stream of smoke billowing from the top chimney. The stillness of the scene against a backdrop of curling smoke is beautiful.

My fear of darkness rears up, but I shove it aside, determined to investigate my surroundings. After the last few days, I'm not taking any chances or blindly assuming everyone else will protect me.

I walk another few yards before somewhere behind me, a branch cracks. It's not loud, but in the silence, it's out of place. I turn, reaching out for the side of the tent for balance.

Nothing moves among the trees, but I spot a shadow that slides to the right, moving stealthily through the cover of branches. My breath catches.

It rounds a fir tree and is almost before me. Suddenly, I'm aware of exactly how exposed and alone I am.

The hooded figure steps out of the shadows into the moonlit space between the forest and the tent at my back.

His broad shoulders take up nearly the entire width between branches, and I can't help but stare at the way his sweatshirt strains against his defined biceps. He's wider than Kol, built like a linebacker.

The man clears his throat to get my attention, and my cheeks heat at the fact that he's busted me for checking him out. My gaze snaps to his, and I find myself trapped in a furious stare of the most startling green eyes I've ever seen.

A very familiar emerald green, in fact.

He pulls back his hood, and I catch sight of his short black hair as he glares at me. I'm tempted to cross my arms in some sort of defense. But since I couldn't possibly have done anything to offend him—yet—and I'm still magic-drunk, I keep my hold on the side of the tent instead.

He doesn't speak.

"If you're looking for Kol, he's devising an exit plan."

His surly expression quickly turns into confusion.

"Kol?"

"Yeah, the protector-dude. Kol."

"He isn't your protector. And I'm not looking for him; I'm looking for you."

"Why?"

"You're Elidi, light goddess ascending."

"And you are?" I ask.

"My name is Helix. I've come to offer myself as your chosen Guardian." He bows stiffly then takes a step toward me, adding, "You're not safe here, Goddess."

Two protectors? No thank you.

"Uh, okay, and where do you propose I go to be safe?" I ask, playing along.

"The Eggther are the only clan divinely ordered for guardianship. You belong in Tegwood with me." He closes the distance between us. "If we hurry, we can slip away before they notice you're gone."

He tries to grab for my wrist.

"Hold it right there," I say, pulling back. "I never said I was going anywhere with you. I've already been kidnapped once today."

"I'm not kidnapping you. I'm your Guardian."

That low voice sends a shiver down my spine, and I

clutch the tent harder, positive it's only for balance and to ward off whatever illness keeps making me pass out. It has nothing to do with how hot this guy is or how tingly his voice makes me feel.

I force myself to focus on what he said.

"Are you a werewolf? Like Kol?"

"We prefer guardian. Or wolf shifter."

I knew I'd seen his green eyes before.

"Fine, wolf *shifter*. Is there something you need?" I ask, haughty in the face of his obvious irritation.

"I need you," he says, and then as if he's realized how his words sound, he swallows hard, and his expression clears, and he adds, "To warn and protect you, I mean."

"Protect me from what?" I ask.

"The Goddess of the Dead has vowed to kill you," he says.

"Whoa there, beastie." I hold up a hand to stop him. "I'm sorry, did you just say the Goddess of the Dead?"

"It is her true title," he says like that should clarify my confusion.

"And what are her false titles?" I ask, hoping he's joking, because if I have the goddess of dead people coming for me, I'm so screwed.

"The Bone Mother, the Daughter of Death, Ruler of The Silenci, Nicnevin." He shrugs. "Not false exactly, but they are some of her other names."

None of those titles sounded remotely better than the first, but her title as Ruler of The Silenci strikes a chord.

"And this Nicnevin person wants to kill me?"

"She's already tried and failed once. But she won't stop until you're dead. You're not safe."

He casts a wary glance left to right as if he's heard something.

"We should go," he says softly.

I stay where I am because no way am I going with this guy. But Helix isn't deterred and simply stares me down with those piercing eyes of his.

"I saw you earlier. Outside the gates. Why were you following us?"

"I was trying to warn you without making a scene," he says quietly.

"Why would you coming here make a scene?" I ask.

"Because I'm not permitted—"

The branches to the side shiver with movement. A second later, a blur of sandy-colored fur flies through, knocking mystery-man clear off his feet. He lands on his back several yards away, and I blink, stunned at the sight of the enormous wolf standing on his chest.

Kol.

He growls down at Helix, but there's no trace of intimidation in those sharp green eyes.

Rage emanates from them both, and I can see the coiling of muscles as they each prepare to attack the other.

A voice cuts through the growling.

"Helix Grigoria."

Vayda appears, practically gliding over the snow in a dress that could have been made from the damn moonlight itself. Her expression is nothing like earlier. The gentle, friendly nursemaid is gone. Instead, her blue eyes glitter like a frozen wasteland, and I can finally see why Kol had been intimidated about coming to visit her.

"Kol, step back," she orders.

Kol's growl stops though his lips remain curled up to reveal his razor-sharp canines. The moment he steps back, Helix gets to his feet. His fists are balled as he glares back at Vayda.

For a moment, I'm thoroughly impressed with Helix's lack of intimidation as Vayda approaches. But some of his confidence melts away as she stops before him.

"You've trespassed on the sacred land of the Vargar. Do you have no regard for the treaty between our people?" she demands in a low voice.

Kol's neighbors begin to arrive, including the floaty red-headed girl I saw on our way in. They stop far outside the circle where Vayda and Helix face off, and no one moves to intervene. If anything, they look wary of Vayda now too.

"I have been divinely ordered to retrieve and protect the goddess ascending," Helix says quietly. There's deference in his tone, but I can still hear the ribbon of anger that runs through it.

"A divine order has no authority here, *Guardian*." Vayda's voice is razor-sharp and lethal. There's something about her relaxed stance and lack of obvious weaponry that makes me wonder what she's really capable of.

"My oath is to the goddess ascending, Lady," Helix says. "I am sworn to do whatever it takes to protect her."

Kol snarls, but Vayda's expression is unmoved.

A figure steps up beside me, and I jump until I see it's Grim.

"What the hell. You gave me a heart attack," I whisper.

Grim wiggles his brows. "I get that a lot."

His hand settles on the small of my back. It feels like a reassurance, and I have no idea for what until Vayda's arm lifts and Helix collapses.

A pained moan escapes Helix, and I take a step forward. Grim's hand snakes around my waist, pulling me back.

I shoot him a fiery look, but his solemn head shake makes me pause.

"You know the law," Vayda says.

The earth shakes beneath my feet at her words. I sway, and Grim's hold around my waist tightens so that I don't fold like an accordion.

Kol glances at me, and our gazes lock for a split second. It's long enough to see that whatever Vayda intends to do to Helix, Kol's more than okay with it. Then his gaze snags on Grim's hand still resting at my hip, and his dark eyes narrow.

"Your punishment is exacted here and now, Eggther," Vayda says.

Helix moans again, clutching at his arm then his stomach. Even though Vayda hasn't moved an inch, I'm positive she's hurting him.

My gaze darts to the others still watching from the shadows. Not one of them moves to stop whatever's happening. Helix cries out again, his agony too much to bear.

"Stop!" My voice echoes sharply, and every single

onlooker turns to me, Vayda included.

Vayda's stare is like granite, and when it lands on me, my legs threaten to give out. Grim's arm is the only thing keeping me upright.

"This is not your concern," she says, her tone icy. Power ripples off of her, and I feel something cold and hard snaking up from my ankles toward my waist.

Grim yanks me against him until I'm crushed to his side.

"Easy, Vayda. She doesn't understand," Grim calls softly.

Vayda's mouth tightens, and her glare switches to Grim. I hold my breath, half-terrified she's about to collapse him too. But then she blinks, and her expression smooths out.

"Take her back to the tent," Vayda says quietly.

"Right away," Grim says.

She turns slowly back to Helix, and I don't miss the gleam in her eye just before she shows me her back. She's enjoying this.

I open my mouth to argue, but Grim lets go of my waist and scoops me into his arms. The only sound I make is a quiet gasp of surprise, and then I'm being carried away from the gathering.

Over Grim's shoulder, I catch sight of Kol staring back at me. Even as a wolf, I can tell he's upset.

I glare steadily back at him, angry and worried for Helix who might have been an ass but certainly doesn't deserve whatever it is they're doing to him now. I open my mouth to yell for them to leave him alone, but the only sound that can be heard over the steel words of Vayda's lecture as she begins torturing him again is

Helix's moan.

CHAPTER EIGHT

GRIM marches into Kol's tent and deposits me unceremoniously onto the bed. I grunt and glare up at him, but his expression silences me.

"Don't fight me on this," he says.

"She's torturing him," I say flatly.

"Vayda is enforcing the laws," Grim says carefully, and it makes me wonder if she can somehow hear us.

"She needs to be stopped."

He sighs. "You don't understand our laws. That guardian knew what he was risking."

"And what about me?"

"What about you?"

"I had no idea what I was getting into. If I break a rule, is she going to torture me too?"

"No," Grim says, and his lips twitch like I've just asked a silly question.

"How can you be so sure?" I ask.

"Because your protector would never let that happen," he says, and there's more certainty in his words than I know what to do with.

Before I can say more, Kol strides in wearing his signature booty shorts. He glowers at me before flicking a quick look at Grim.

Without a word, Grim backs away from the bed. When he doesn't leave, though, I wonder if he's protecting Kol or me.

I use what remaining strength I have to sit up.

"Helix doesn't deserve torture," I say to Kol.

"He knew the rules when he came here."

"All he did was come talk to me. What sort of rule does that violate?"

Kol's expression turns stony.

"He trespassed on Vargar land. The penalty for an Eggther trespassing here is severe. Trust me. He got off easy."

"You wish Vayda had hurt him more." It's not a question. "Why do you hate him so much?"

"It's complicated." He stalks away and begins stuffing a few more items into the bags at the door.

"Look, I'm new to this, okay? Obviously there's a lot I don't understand, but that won't change if you don't talk to me."

He doesn't respond, and it's ridiculous, but I know he's mad at me for what happened with Helix.

"Protecting me should include educating me about the shit I step in, you know."

"You have to tell her," Grim says quietly.

Kol turns on him, glaring.

"Now," Grim adds, clearly not intimidated by an angry Kol. "Before you take her out into the world. She needs to know. You need to build trust if this is going to work."

The urge to ask what he's talking about is strong, but I manage to keep quiet while Kol and Grim face off.

Finally, Kol sighs, running a hand through his messy hair.

"Fine."

Grim's eyes twinkle triumphantly as he looks over at me.

"Helix is a Guardian, but he belongs to the Eggther pack," Kol says.

"And your packs don't get along?" I say.

Grim snorts, but Kol ignores him and says, "You could say we're rivals."

"Why?" I ask.

"It's kind of a long story."

"You should get comfortable," Grim adds.

They both wait, watching me expectantly, so I make a point to snuggle in against the pillows at my back. When I'm done, Kol crosses his arms and stands beside the bed.

"To understand, it's best to go back to the beginning. A thousand years ago, there was a war between the gods. Between brothers, actually. Zeus and Hades had always been rivals, always competing, always trying to outdo the other."

"Wait. Hades as in the god of the Underworld?" I ask.

Kol nods, utterly serious. "When the brothers were old enough to reign, Zeus was given the heavens, and Hades was given Hell. But Hades resented his birthright. He went to Zeus to ask for a more even split of power, but Zeus refused him. From that point on, it became about building an army—or at least it was for

Hades. Fighting broke out, and it escalated until war spread. The heavens were a battlefield, and the fighting eventually spilled over into the human world where Zeus sent some of his children to hide. Heracles. Athena. You've heard some of their names already. Anyway, Hades found them and, one by one, he slaughtered them."

"Holy shit, Athena? Are all the myths real then?" I ask.

Grim chuckles.

Kol shrugs. "Gods, goddesses—and the wolves that protect them. We're all real."

"Oh and demons," Grim puts in. "Don't forget Hades' kids."

"Demons are the children of a god?" I ask.

"You can call them hellions if you want, but yes," Kol says.

"The Great War went on for decades, and Hades slowly began to gain the upper hand. Gods and goddesses were being killed in staggering numbers. The Eggther, their wolf protectors, were losing numbers faster than the pack could replenish their ranks. They were losing the war. Zeus feared for the extinction of our kind, so he went to Odin and struck a bargain. Odin would create the Vargar, a new breed of Guardian wolves to help fight alongside the gods and the Eggther."

"So, everyone here is descended from Odin?" I ask. He nods. "And what about Vayda? Is she Odin's descendant too?"

"No. Vayda is Odin's consort." At my expression, he explains, "Sort of like his wife."

"So she really is your mother?" I ask.

"Not exactly. Odin didn't mix his bloodline for us. We were created using his god-magic."

I snicker. "That sounds vague. Kind of like the stork brought you here."

Grim snorts.

Kol rolls his eyes. "Gods are, at their core, creators of worlds, Elidi. Odin can create without intercourse." He pauses, probably to see if I'll interrupt, but there are way too many questions to pick just one. He goes on, "Odin doesn't take part in this realm. It was part of his deal with Zeus that he remain removed from his creations. When the war ended, Odin sent Vayda to take us in."

"That's why you call her your stepmother," I say, and they both nod. "Who are the Eggther descended from?"

"Lycaon, a son of Zeus, was the first Guardian," Kol says. "He was killed in the war while protecting humans from Hades' legion."

"I don't get it. If both clans are guardians of the gods, why banish you? Why can't you work together? You're doing the same thing."

Kol and Grim exchange a look, and I know even before they answer that it's not that simple.

"After the Vargar joined Zeus and his army, Hades and his demons were driven back to Hell. The war ended. We'd won as a united people. But the Eggther became resentful of us. Zeus ordered that the Eggther were the only chosen guardians. From then on, only Eggther could be tasked with protecting the gods and goddesses. The Vargar were cast out. No longer recognized as true guardians."

"That's terrible," I say. "Why would they do that?"

"With the gods, it's always been about purity of bloodlines. Even Vayda isn't recognized as a true goddess on this plane because she was created to rule in another realm."

"That's ridiculous," I say. "Vayda's terrifying. I have a feeling she could convince them to change their minds if she tried."

Kol shrugs. "Vayda's content with her place in the world."

"For now," Grim adds, and it makes me wonder what he knows.

But Kol brushes it off and goes on. "We came here and built a home for ourselves in Black Peak. With Vayda's help, a treaty was drawn up between our two packs that expressly forbids trespassing by a member of the other clan. This has been the only thing to keep the peace for a century. The mongrel from earlier—"

"Helix," I say.

Kol's expression darkens at my use of his name, but he continues as if I hadn't interrupted him. "He came here knowing it would violate the treaty. He took that risk."

"He thinks you shouldn't protect me," I say.

Kol's eyes flash with instant fury.

"It's none of his business," he snaps.

"Kol," Grim says, a warning edge to his voice.

"What that mutt meant is that I'm not *allowed* to protect you."

"Because you're not recognized by the gods as an official guardian," I say.

Kol nods. His gaze is intense on mine, and I know he's waiting for my full reaction to this.

"But you're going to do it anyway," I say.

"I told you about the visions I've had," he says. "They were unrelenting. The only way to stop them was to come to you. Believe me. I tried not to. I really did try to stay away and let the Eggther handle it. But I couldn't. And you should be glad for that. On the night you were attacked, no Eggther came to your aid. You'd be dead or worse if I hadn't come."

"Why me?" I ask.

"You're important, Elidi," he says, and a ripple of pleasure goes through me at his words. "With your mother gone, you're the only light goddess left in the six realms. I have a feeling whoever tried to hurt you isn't going to stop, and I have to trust that whatever sent me to you did it because you need me more than you need an Eggther."

"Nicnevin," I say, and both men go still.

"What?" Grim says.

"Helix told me that's who attacked my aunt Aerina. That's who's after me."

"That Helix guy is really starting to piss me off." Grim shoves off the wall and marches closer, casting wary looks at Kol as he approaches. "Do you think he's right?"

"Explains the army," Kol says quietly.

"What army?" I ask.

But Kol answers with a question of his own. "How does he know she's the one after you?"

"We didn't get that far before we were interrupted," I say.

Grim snickers, and Kol glares at him. "Well, you did make a rather dramatic entrance."

"What the hell does the Bone Mother want with Elidi?" Grim asks.

Kol sits on the bed beside me.

"If the Eggther is right, that means we need to get you somewhere safe. Nicnevin is powerful and has eyes everywhere."

"First, this was supposed to be somewhere safe," I say. "Second, I'm not going anywhere until you tell me what army you're talking about."

When Kol doesn't immediately answer, I summon what little energy I have left to lean forward and poke a finger in his chest.

"I thought we were past the secrecy. Full disclosure, remember?"

"The Silenci," Kol says. "They're meant to guard the Underworld. Hades rules them, but technically, they follow a blood link. Nicnevin could have established herself as their general. It explains why they're hunting you."

"But why would this woman want to kill me at all?" I demand. "What did I do to her?"

"No idea," Kol admits. "Maybe it has to do with your mom."

I blink, completely taken aback by that answer. "She died last year," I say quietly.

"Which means she would have passed through Gehenna," Grim points out.

"And Gehenna is?" I ask.

"The Underworld. And that's Nicnevin's arena, so maybe they didn't hit it off." Kol runs a hand through his hair. "I wish I'd gotten a closer look before we jumped. Maybe I would have seen her before we crossed over."

"Crossed over?" I repeat then I remember the river. "Right. When you kidnapped me. Which we still need to talk about by the way."

"You kidnapped her?" Grim asks, brows lifting.

Kol scowls. "No, I didn't kidnap her." He turns to me. "I saved you, remember? A job that's proving harder and harder the longer I know you."

"Bite me," I mutter.

Grim barks out a laugh, and I watch as a flush creeps up Kol's neck into his cheeks, turning his entire face a bright red.

"What?" I ask.

"Nothing," Kol mutters. He stands and ducks away from me, shoving Grim with his shoulder, and I know I've just said something wrong. But neither one offers to explain, and when Kol turns around again, he looks somewhat recovered.

"I'm going off script by protecting you, Elidi. I'm not going to lie and tell you this will work out for either of us, but I can promise you that I'm not going to let anything happen to you out there. I'll die before I let anyone hurt you."

His words feel enormous, and I try to remember if I've ever been promised something so meaningful before.

"Thank you," I say. "And I believe that you'll keep your word."

He reaches for my hand and wraps it in his.

"We have to leave Black Peak," he says. And the

way he searches my eyes with his makes it all feel like a question. Like he's asking me if this is okay. Like we really are planning it together. A team.

"You're too weak to survive behind the veil. The Earth plane is dangerous now, but I know somewhere we can go while you wait for your ascension."

"One condition," I say as if I'm in any kind of position to make demands.

"Name it," Kol says.

"Teach me." I look from him to Grim. "Show me how to ascend or be a goddess or whatever. And if you don't know how I can do that, then train me. I need to do more than run away and hide where I'm safe when shit hits the fan. I have to be able to find Aerina, and if there's any chance of saving her, I have to do that too."

Kol looks back at Grim. "Do you think she'll let you get away?" Kol asks.

I frown, wondering who they're talking about.

Grim nods gravely. "I'll need some time to set it up. Where should I meet you?"

"We'll go to the Wryneck," Kol says, a strange note in his voice.

Grim's brows shoot up. "Do you think that's wise?"

Kol shrugs. "It's safest. That's what matters."

Grim glances at me with an interest that makes me shift in my seat. What the hell is a wryneck? Before I can ask, Kol turns back to me, and his jaw is set.

"Grim will meet us there once he's made his own arrangements. He's the best option for your goddess training."

Both of them fall silent, waiting for my answer.

"Okay," I say. "I'll go with you."

"Really?" Kol blinks, clearly surprised. "Damn, that was easier than I thought."

"You've proven already that you can protect me. I'm alive because of you. Besides, I'm really tired of this magical narcolepsy thing, so it's not like I can stay here anyway." I yawn and catch sight of Kol's smile and Grim's barely contained laughter. "But can we wait until after my nap? I'm really tired of waking up in new places."

The last thing I hear before I drift off is Kol's laughter and the words, "No promises on that one."

CHAPTER NINE

I wake to sunlight and enough jostling that I groan as I sit up. Kol has obviously disregarded my last request. I look down at the leather strap fastened low over my lap. A lap that is still clothed in the leggings and tunic from before. At least I haven't been undressed again, so that's something.

"You lied," I mumble, exhaustion robbing the words of venom.

Underneath me, Kol's shoulders shake with laughter.

Actually, I promised nothing.

"Ass," I say, which only makes him laugh harder. "Where are we?"

Almost there, he replies in my head.

"Where is there?"

No answer.

I open my mouth to blast him for sucky manners when a gust of wind blows through the treetops at our backs. Panic rises, leaving a bitter taste in the back of my throat. The last time the wind swept in like this, it had ushered an army toward us.

Kol turns his head to get a look at the sky.

Just like before, the leaves shake, and branches sway as the wind rushes by. My hair blows into my eyes, and I shove it back with a weak hand. My breath shortens with the simple movement, and I realize we must still be in Black Peak if I'm this run-down.

My fear subsides a little. "Whatever's out there can't get to us in here," I whisper. "Right?"

They're beyond the gates, Kol says. *Waiting.*

"Is there another way out?" I ask. "A different—"

My question goes unanswered as the wind suddenly sends a tree crashing toward the forest floor— its thick trunk aimed right for us. Kol launches sideways, narrowly avoiding being smashed. Leaves fly, wind howls, and Kol's powerful body races along the ground at an impossible speed.

On our right, dark shadows move through the trees, running parallel to us. They don't move closer as they keep pace, and I barely have time to wonder what's keeping them back when I catch sight of a pair of iron gates up ahead. They stand wide open, but nothing's rushing the entrance. Whatever's tracking us remains outside—a fact that does nothing to comfort me since we're headed right for the opening. Right for *them.*

A scream sounds, and its ear-piercing octave is one I recognize immediately.

The Silenci

Nicnevin.

Goddess of the Dead.

She's here.

"It's Nic—"

I know.

Even in my head, Kol's tone is like steel—hard and determined and focused on the path ahead as we bound closer and closer to the gated opening before us. These gates are different than the ones we passed through on our way in, but there's no time to ask why or where they lead.

Just beyond, shadows loom. Winged creatures whose hooves don't quite touch the ground. Red eyes stare back at me from where they've gathered to wait for us. Even though they've stopped, the wind continues to spin around me, urging us closer.

"Kol," I yell, desperate now and wide awake thanks to the gallons of adrenaline my body is circulating.

Ten more steps.

Eight.

Six.

The gate is so close now.

The monsters, the red eyes—

"Kol!" I scream.

Hold on!

His voice is a command and a warning and gives me only enough time to bury my fists in his thick fur before he leaps.

I shut my eyes and am shocked when several seconds pass and Kol's paws have yet to touch the ground.

I open my eyes, braced for the worst. But nothing waits for us as we finish our leap. The shadows are gone, and by the time Kol's paws touch down again, the scenery before us has completely shifted. The forest is gone. In its place is a dirt path wide enough to be some kind of farming road. It's deserted and winding upward with low shrubs growing along either side. The chill has suddenly become a melting heat, and the sun hangs behind the mountain that rises up before us.

My confusion becomes awe as Kol continues to run, winding up and around the mountain road where we've landed.

I twist hard to look behind us, fully expecting to see the red-eyed monsters pursuing us. But there's nothing. No shadows. No glowing eyes. No wind.

We're alone. But most importantly, we're safe.

"What the hell just happened?" I ask on a deep breath that's meant to test whether or not I'm actually alive.

The Silenci were waiting for us. I had to veil-jump again. How do you feel?

I can feel the weight of my exhaustion as my adrenaline rush fades.

"Tired," I admit. If he tells me to go to sleep again just so he can transport me somewhere else I haven't asked to go—

I couldn't avoid it. Not with The Silenci waiting for us. It'll pass now that we're back on the earth plane.

I hope he's right.

Kol steps off the path and comes to a stop.

"What are we doing?" I ask.

Kol reaches back with his teeth and pulls on the end of the strap buckling me in, releasing me. Before I can catch myself, I slide off and land in a heap on the ground beside him.

Kol makes a strange growly noise in his throat that sounds suspiciously like a laugh.

I sit up, rubbing at the places where sharp gravel has dug into my skin, and glare.

"I thought you said your job was to protect me."

Kol takes another step back, and then his fur begins to shimmer, and his body trembles. I blink at a sudden small flash of light, and when I open my eyes again, Kol looks human.

My eyes dip lower to his broad, bared chest and the tiny shorts that cover yet highlight his most impressive part.

Kol clears his throat.

My eyes snap back to his, and I don't miss the gleam he wears. My cheeks heat. So busted.

I scramble to my feet and busy myself with combing dirty fingers through my crazy hair. Kol reaches for the bag that's now on the ground beside me and produces a candy bar from one of the pockets.

"Here," he says. "Eat this. It'll help with the exhaustion from the veil-jump."

I rip into it, silently fighting the urge to kiss him on the mouth for the chocolate. "So now you're back to taking care of me again?" I ask around a mouthful of milk chocolate and caramel.

"I never said I'd take care of you. I said I'd protect you. Totally different."

I roll my eyes. "Tomato, potato."

He cocks his head and opens his mouth then apparently thinks better of it and shuts it again.

"Eat up," he says finally. "We have a bit of a walk."

"Bossy much?" I take another bite.

He scoops up the bag and then looks at me, one brow arched. My stomach flips, and I silently curse myself for how much I like looking at him.

"Actually, I'm doing that protector thing," he says. "We're in the desert, and the sun's rising high, which means it's going to be hot as Hades very soon. I'd like to spare us both from heat exhaustion if you don't mind."

"Can werewolves get heat exhaustion?" I ask.

"I am not a werewolf," he says tightly, and I hide my smile by shoving what's left of the candy bar into my mouth.

"Right, sorry," I say around the mouthful of sugary goodness. "Can *guardians* get heat exhaustion? I mean, don't you heal quickly from injuries?"

"How do you know that?" he asks.

I shrug. "Your ear was hurt during the fight, but when you came out of the river, it was healed."

His eyes narrow. "You noticed that all by yourself?"

I roll my eyes. "I'm not a complete idiot." He snorts, and I glare. "Is it some kind of secret or something?" I demand.

"No. Yes. Sort of." He sighs. "Crossing into Black Peak is good for my wolf side. It's healing and gives me a kind of a boost to be where my pack's magic is so strong. But yes, even outside the borders of Black Peak, we heal faster than humans. And gods."

"See?" I shoot back. "Was that so hard?"

Kol turns and starts walking.

He's headed in the opposite direction of the road, and I have to hurry to catch up.

For the next few minutes, we walk in silence. The

sun beats down on my head, and a light sheen of sweat begins to coat my skin.

Without breaking stride, I peel off the tunic to reveal the thin tank top underneath. The sweat coating me has plastered both the shirt and the leggings to my damp skin, but it's slightly cooler without the tunic on.

"You should leave it," Kol says, and I catch him side-eying me. "The tunic will help keep the sun's rays off so you don't burn."

"I don't burn anyway," I tell him. "Never have."

He doesn't look convinced, but he doesn't argue.

I tie the tunic around my head to cool my hair, and we continue on.

On either side of us, the dusty landscape is open and arid, dotted only with low-lying shrubs and cacti stretching as far as I can see. The only good thing about our surroundings is the lack of glowing-eyed monsters.

Kol's gaze is watchful and constantly scanning though I have no idea if he's looking for a threat or for some sign we're actually going in the right direction. Everything looks the same to me.

"Where are we going?" I ask when my legs ache and the silence has become loud between us.

"To see a friend," he says.

At his succinct answer, I glance over and see the sweat coating his chest and arms. His cheeks are flushed, and his hair is wet and slicked back from running his hand through it. Every inch of his exposed skin is bronzed and chiseled and glistening. It's a trifecta that makes me drool the little bit of moisture I have left in my mouth.

He looks over, and I quickly look away again. What

was I saying?

"The Wryneck?" I ask. Kol cuts me a surprised look, and I sigh. "Again, not an idiot. Also, you and Grim talk in front of me like I'm not even there."

"Yes," he says. "Her name is Iynx. She's a goddess with an affinity for protection borders. Her property is ringed in an impenetrable shield, which means even if our enemies find us, they won't be able to get inside."

"Huh. Seems like a smart move." His brows lift, and I realize he wasn't looking for my praise. Whatever. "How did they know where to find us anyway?" I ask. "The Silenci waiting at the gate, I mean."

"They probably caught our trail before it disappeared into the river. I'm guessing they put sentries on all gates leading away from Black Peak and just waited."

"Wait. Does that mean they'll find our trail here?"

"They'll look for it. But we're a thousand miles away. That veil-jump should mask us at least long enough to reach Iynx. Once we cross her barrier, we'll be safe."

"Does this barrier involve crossing another veil?" I ask.

"No. Iynx's barrier is more earth-magic than god-gifted," Kol says.

"Right. Obviously," I agree as if I understand any of what he's talking about. He shoots me a glance.

"Earth-magic is something the human world is tapped into. It calls upon the favor of a god or goddess to activate, but it's not otherworldly. It still adheres to the laws of this dimension, which means your mortal body won't have a reaction to it."

"I still don't understand how I'm allergic to god-magic if I am one."

"You're a goddess ascending. It's different. And you're not allergic."

"So you all keep saying"

"You're only mortal until you ascend. Ascension means coming into your power. It also means leaving your mortality behind."

"Whoa. Hold the flip up." I stop and stare at him. "Do you mean that once I ascend, I'll be *immortal*?"

Kol stops and faces me. "Yes. You're a goddess, Elidi. That means you'll live forever."

"Wow." I take a moment to let that sink in then ask, "Are Guardians immortal too?"

Kol blinks then looks away. "Guardians become immortal when they become bonded."

"Okay," I say, when he doesn't say more. "And your bonded half is...?"

"No one. At least not yet," he says. Then he clears his throat and rubs the back of his neck awkwardly.

I cock my head. "Did I step in some shit again?"

His brows crinkle. "What?"

"What did I just say? And why does it feel awkward? Look, I don't know what any of this means, Wolf-man. That's what I have you for, remember? So you can't—"

"Wolf-man?" he repeats, arching a brow.

I shrug. "Yeah. So?"

"That's . . . what? Your nickname for me?"

I nod.

"You couldn't come up with something better than that?"

"Wolf-man's very manly," I say, grinning.

I start walking again, vaguely aware he's just avoided answering my questions. But maybe one batshit crazy truth at a time is enough.

I'm immortal.

Or I will be.

Suddenly, I'm the one who needs a distraction.

"Fine. What do you want me to call you?" I ask.

He slants a look at me as we walk on. "How about Guardian Hotness? Or Ninja Warrior Wolf?"

My nose wrinkles. "Those are even worse than Wolf-man."

He grins. "They're more inclusive of my skills though."

I roll my eyes. "Your only skills are running really fast and being grumpy. Maybe I should call you Fast and Furious."

His confusion only makes that funnier, and I double over, laughing hard at his expression.

"That's ridiculous," he says, obviously clueless.

"Don't worry. It's also already taken," I say then wipe my forehead.

"I'm not trying to suggest you do all the hard work in this partnership, but if you were a wolf right now, we could run across this desert, and we'd be there by now."

"First, that's not a suggestion. It's a fact. I've done all the work so far. You've merely survived."

I stick my tongue out. "Surviving is hard."

He chuckles. "For you, that is probably true," he says, and I glare back at him. "But for your information, I can't cross Iynx's barrier as a wolf. The magic won't allow it."

"Why won't it—"

Something thick and jelly-like hits me. It's invisible and not quite solid enough to stop my forward momentum. As I pass through it with a half-open mouth, whatever the substance is fills my mouth. I come out the other side, back into real air, and heave up the invisible contents coating my tongue.

A wad of jelly-like spit hits the ground—yellowish and no longer invisible.

"Ugh. Ew. Gross." My stomach rolls at the aftertaste. I bend at the knees, spitting into the dirt again and again. "I might be sick. What the hell *was* that?"

"Plsdntbskhlp." Kol's voice is muffled.

I turn to see his arms and legs frozen in mid-stride. His nose is mashed against some sort of invisible wall, and I can see the muscles in his biceps contracting as he tries to pull free of whatever has him locked in place. It's not working.

He tries to call out again. "Ldigrbmahhndnpll."

I snort, which is much better than the knee-slapping laughter that wants to come out.

"Do you want my help?" I ask, stepping closer.

Kol tries to nod, but his forehead and chin are frozen in place.

"But I'm only good at surviving, remember?"

He glares at me, and I cover my mouth to hold the laughter inside.

"Nthlpng." Kol's voice, though still muffled, is irritated enough that I bite my lips and step forward.

Slowly, I reach out and grasp his hand. Just like before, the jelly-like barrier slides around my skin, and

I cringe at the wrongness of it. Especially when there's nothing to see.

"How are you stuck in this when it's so gooey and soft?" I ask.

But Kol only grunts an answer.

His fingers twitch toward mine, and I shove my hand farther inside then wrap it around his wrist and pull. He doesn't budge, and I begin to wonder if I'm even strong enough to get him out.

I tug again, harder this time, and there's a suction-y popping sound as the jelly turns to liquid, releasing Kol more suddenly than either of us is ready for.

He bumps into me as he falls, taking me with him.

I grunt as my back hits the ground, and Kol lands on top of me. The jelly or liquid or whatever it is has vanished, and now there's only my skin against his.

Kol's gaze captures mine, and his expression darkens. My belly heats, creating a tingle and a shudder that goes all the way through me. Without thought, I lift my hand and press it to his cheek then slide it around to the back of his neck.

His skin is slick, and I can feel the layer of dust that coats him underneath the sweat. It should be a complete turn-off, but instead, it's dirty in a way that has me licking my lips in anticipation.

Kol leans down and presses his mouth against mine. My eyelids shudder closed, and explosions go off behind them. The pleasure rocks me, and I grab hold of him with both hands, hanging on for dear life.

Kol's mouth moves slowly as if he's savoring the taste of my lips. I press harder against him, pulling him to me because even though we're already pressed together from mouth to feet, it's not enough.

I want more.

Dizziness washes over me in waves, and I hear myself moan. It sounds strange to me, like another version of myself that I've only now just met. But I've never been kissed before. Not like this, anyway. And not by a—

A pain explodes in my head, spearing through my skull from temple to temple. Kol wrenches his mouth away from mine, but my arms are locked around his neck against the debilitating pain.

Death by kissing. There are worse ways to go.

Above me, Kol groans, and I have to assume he's under the same sort of attack I am. Hopefully, he's not *this* disappointed with our kiss.

He reaches up and pries my hands apart then rolls off me, coming to all fours in the dirt.

"Fuck, Iynx, ease up," Kol says through clenched teeth. "It's me."

At his words, the pain in my head disappears.

"Kol Valco," a woman says. "Is that really you?"

I pry my eyes open to look at the woman standing over us. The sexy fitted gown she wears displays her impressive breasts as she aims her cat-like smile at Kol. Her long brown hair, tied back in a braid that dangles nearly to her ass, sways as she steps toward him.

She doesn't even seem to notice me as I sit up.

Kol rolls back onto his heels and cuts her a look.

"Do you have another guardian friend stupid enough to walk into your wards?"

She grins and grabs Kol's shoulder, hauling him up for a fierce hug complete with neck kisses and wandering hands. I pretend the streak of jealousy racing through me is just suspicion. By the time they break apart, I'm on my feet and watching them with my arms folded as I count all the things that are probably wrong with her as a trade-off for being so pretty. I'm up to serial farter when Kol turns to me and says my name. Yep, definitely just suspicion.

"Elidi, this is Iynx. Iynx, this is Elidi, daughter of Hemera, my sworn."

I paste a smile on my face and extend my hand, but Iynx ignores it, her gaze whipping to Kol.

"You have a light goddess ascending for a sworn?" she demands, and I can't tell if she's angry or just "suspicious" of me—like I am of her.

"The visions came to me," he says quietly. "And so, I made the oath."

Iynx gasps. "Does Vayda know? Does the Eggther?"

"Yes." Kol's expression offers more, and I watch as Iynx studies him for a long moment.

Shadows cross her flawless face before she finally turns back to me, and a slow smile spreads. She reaches for me with both hands, wrapping hers around mine. I wonder if it matters that I'm covered in sweat and dust and whatever residue that invisible barrier is made of, but she doesn't seem to notice or care.

"Elidi, I am so pleased to meet you. I'm sure you want to get out of the sun and get cleaned up. Please, come." She lets go of my hands and places hers on my shoulder, guiding me back the way she came.

I falter when I catch sight of the connected buildings before us. The two structures are a mix of wood and glass done in clean, contemporary lines with solar panels covering the main roof. A gravel walkway lined with pavers leads from the main door to the smaller building with a breezeway connecting the two.

"Was that there the whole time?" I ask.

Iynx pats my shoulder, urging me forward again. "The barrier conceals it. You can't see it until you've passed through."

"You mean the invisible jelly wall?" I ask.

Kol snorts and Iynx smiles knowingly. "It felt that way to you because you're mortal. A Guardian would have felt something much thicker."

"That's why he got stuck in it," I realize.

She nods. "It would have continued to solidify until it became like cement, crushing his airways until he died." She sounds very satisfied with the possibility, and I look at her, horrified.

"Your mortality saved him. Good thing he was in his human form too," she adds.

"What would happen if he wasn't?" I ask.

"Earth magic repels god magic," she says. "The stronger the god magic, the stronger the repulsion."

"It gets a little explodey," Kol says, clarifying.

I shudder, and Iynx laughs lightly.

"Here we are," she says, way too cheerful considering the subject matter.

We stop in front of a glass door of the smaller building. Through the window, I catch sight of a cozy sitting area done in earthy tones and furnished with half a dozen deep-cushioned chairs.

"This is the guest house. Inside, you'll find everything you need, so please make yourself at home. I assume you two would like to get cleaned up," Iynx says.

I nod eagerly.

"Elidi, you'll sleep in the bedroom here, and you can shower in the attached bathroom."

"Thank you," I say, grateful for the modern accommodations after the tents of Black Peak.

"There are towels and soaps already stocked for you," she says. "I'd give you the grand tour, but it's been a while since I've had visitors, and my hunger's a little hard to quell just now."

She turns a sultry gaze toward Kol. "Darling?" she says, hooking her finger into the waistline of his shorts. "Care to join me?"

Heat rushes up my throat and into my cheeks, and I don't wait for him to reply before I push my way inside the guest house.

At my back, Kol says something too low for me to hear.

Iynx practically purrs at him in response, and a red cloud blurs my vision. I kick the front door shut and march across the pristine living space.

The bedroom is soft and inviting with a white down comforter and throw pillows that match the artwork hanging, all of it done in splashes of burnt oranges and browns. Opposite the bed, two large windows look out over the desert, gauzy white curtains hanging over both. I turn away from them, barely seeing any of it in my haze of fury, and march past a shiny turquoise dresser into the bathroom.

Just inside, I stop and stare.

Some of my rage dissipates, and I wonder if it's

even possible to be this angry and this excited at the same time.

I haven't had a bathroom this big ever.

A whirlpool tub complete with jets sits on a raised platform in the far corner, the entire dais encased in Spanish tile. A standup shower with heads on all three walls stands beside that, and on my right are double sinks and a counter top large enough to act out the entire bar scene from Coyote Ugly.

It even smells fancy. I note the essential oil diffuser already going in the corner of the open shelving beside the tub.

Had Iynx known we were coming? The thought just stirs my anger back to life.

"An angry bath," I mutter aloud. "That's what I'll take."

I decide to try my best to be multi-talented enough to both enjoy this haven and be pissed at my hostess and her shower-buddy. Maybe I'll even use all the hot water just to spite the *lovers* in the big house.

"Kol's a horrible kisser," I say, repeating it to myself while I soak in bubble bath bliss.

Forty-five minutes later, I finally pull myself out of the water and wrap a towel around myself before heading back to the guest bedroom to look for clean clothes.

The moment I open the door, I spot Kol standing by the bed and yelp, scrambling back a step. My tenuous tuck of my towel loosens. Before I can grab it, the towel falls to the ground at my feet.

My eyes snap to Kol's.

His gaze takes in everything I've just put on

display. My skin prickles, and my nipples harden; and I hate that, for a split second, I don't even want to cover up.

Then I notice that he's exchanged his shorts for a fresh pair of sweats, and his hair drips at the ends, freshly washed and uncombed. And I remember that he's come from doing God-knows-what with Iynx—right after making out with me moments before.

Heat floods my face, and I dive for the towel before retreating back into the bathroom. I slam the door between us. My breaths are labored as I cinch the towel even tighter around my body this time.

A quick glance in the mirror shows my wet, tangled hair falling over bony shoulders and framing a beet-red face. Not exactly on par with the seductress whose bathtub I'm borrowing.

There's a soft knock on the door.

"You okay?" Kol asks, and there's just enough amusement in his voice to make me more furious than embarrassed.

I march over and fling the door wide open, glaring back at him.

"I'm fine."

"Well, you look great," he says with a cocky smile.

I swing my hand out, but he dances out of reach before it can connect.

"Whoa, there. It's not my fault you can't keep a towel on."

"I realize this isn't the first time today you've been faced with a naked woman, but try to recognize I'm not using the opportunity to proposition you."

His expression darkens.

"Elidi . . ." He trails off.

"What?" I demand, but it's lost its bite because now, all I can think of is the way he kissed me earlier.

Kol's stormy gray gaze swirls with all the things he isn't saying out loud.

"What?" I repeat.

He looks to where I clutch the towel then he blinks, and I know I've lost him to whatever thoughts he's battling.

"Help yourself to whatever's in the closet," he says quietly. "Iynx is bringing food and drink when you're ready."

Without waiting for an answer, he turns and walks out. I watch him go, frowning at his stiff shoulders until he disappears.

Horrible kisser, I remind myself, but the lie's too empty to believe.

CHAPTER TEN

IYNX is waiting when I emerge, fully clothed and hair brushed. On the end table beside her is a tray with a pitcher full of something pink and an assortment of cookies. My stomach growls at the sight of the food, and I find myself torn between wanting to claw Iynx's eyes out and wanting to kiss her.

"That dress fits you perfectly," she says with a smile as I cross to where she waits.

"Thanks."

My hands come up to smooth the flowy green skirt that billows out from an empire waist. It's way too fancy for daywear, but it was the most casual dress in the closet. The only other options had been lingerie, which I assume belongs to Iynx.

"Lemonade?" she asks, pouring a glass.

"Thank you." I accept the drink and don't bother with polite sips. Instead, I gulp half the pink goodness before coming up for air.

Iynx laughs. "I'm sorry. I should have offered you water before your shower."

"No, this is great." It was more than great. It was delicious.

Iynx motions to the chairs by the window.

"Why don't we sit? I'd love to hear about your trip."

I sink into a chair, watching Iynx warily now. Whatever she wants to know, I'm sure Kol can fill her in. Unless they didn't do much talking. The lemonade in my stomach turns sour at the thought.

"Where's Kol?" I ask.

"He went to get some air," she says.

My eyes narrow. I doubt she's telling the truth since we both had plenty of air on the two-hour walk here. But I don't say anything, instead taking another sip.

"You should know that he and I did not have sex earlier," she says.

I nearly spray lemonade all over her silky maxi dress.

"What?" I ask when I finally manage to swallow.

"Kol and I didn't—"

"Yeah, I heard you. I mean, why are you telling me?"

She shrugs. "Because it matters to you. Because you want to have sex with him."

"Whoa, I think you have the wrong idea."

She cocks her head at me. "Do I?"

"Yes. You know most people don't just come right out and start throwing around words like 'sex,' especially if they've just met."

Iynx wiggles her eyebrows. "They do with me."

Her complete confidence leaves no doubt that she's

probably telling the truth.

"Well, Kol and I are not having sex. Nor do we plan to have sex. He's my guardian. My protector. Nothing more."

She leans forward, showcasing the top half of her breasts that are nearly spilling from her dress.

"Elidi, I would never betray your desires. Those belong to you, and only you can voice those to Kol or anyone else. I'm not going to say anything. I just wanted you to know that I see Kol isn't free to pleasure me any longer."

She leans back again, adding, "And I respect that."

"You don't have very good people skills, do you?"

"On the contrary. I am very skilled with people." Her lips curve seductively. "Especially with pleasuring those people."

My eyes widen. "Are you hitting on me?"

Iynx laughs, and it's a real, honest belly laugh that puts me at ease while still somehow managing to turn me on.

"No, darling. Well, not unless it's working." She winks.

"Uh, no thank you." My cheeks heat, and I cover my embarrassment by finishing off the last of my lemonade.

"Did Kol not tell you anything about me?"

"He said you were a friend and that your magic works with my mortal body so, you know, it won't kill me while keeping us safe from the demon unicorns."

"The Silenci." Iynx's smile fades. "Yes, Kol told me about your fan club. I'm so sorry. Aerina is a friend, and I hate to hear of her suffering."

"You know my aunt?" I sit up straighter and set my glass aside, eager for Iynx's answer.

Iynx hesitates briefly then says, "Aerina and I spent some time together several years back." Something about the way she says it, so careful, makes me wonder what brought them together. And what tore them apart. But Iynx goes on, "I have to say I'm surprised to hear Nicnevin is behind what happened. This is not like her at all."

"Kol says she's the Goddess of the Dead. I mean, based on the title alone, what's to be surprised about?"

Iynx shakes her head. "Nicnevin's role isn't about causing harm; it's about shepherding souls. She has access to the underworld as well as the celestial afterlife, and she doesn't take that responsibility lightly."

"What sort of celestial afterlife? You mean like Heaven?"

"Well, it's not quite the human version you've heard about, but yes, essentially. Nicnevin escorts the souls of the dead into the realm they've earned when their mortal life ends. But she's not violent."

"Well, she made an exception for Aerina," I mutter darkly.

"It's a very interesting story," she murmurs.

I study her, a little irritated. "It's more than a story, and it's terrifying, actually. Aerina is my only family, and now she's gone. On top of that, I have to ascend, whatever that means, and find a way to defeat Nicnevin so I can save my aunt. Interesting doesn't really cover it."

"Of course, Elidi, I didn't mean to dismiss your

situation," Iynx says. "Forgive me. This feud with Nicki isn't something I take lightly."

"Nicki?" I repeat. "Wait. You know her? Personally?"

"She's come to me before."

The way she says it holds meaning I can't quite grasp. Whatever it is has Iynx's mouth curving again in that same secret, seductive smile she used on me earlier.

"What would she come to you for exactly?"

"For sex," she says as if the answer's obvious.

I clear my throat. "Okay, I'm not judging here. Just trying to understand. Are you saying you and Nicnevin hook up?"

"Yes, occasionally. I am the Goddess of Pleasure, darling. My gifts work best on those who need the kind of companionship only a physical union can provide. Sometimes, I match others together, and sometimes I provide pleasure myself."

I stare at her, speechless, as her words sink slowly into my shocked brain. "Like a madam or something?"

"Oh, what I do is so much more than a madam, Elidi. Come here. Let me show you." She stands and offers her hand.

Against my better judgment, my hand reaches for hers and slides over her smooth skin.

Iynx pulls me to my feet and guides me to the window until I'm standing before the glass with Iynx behind me. She points to a figure outside.

"Look at him," she says softly, her words unnecessary because I can't seem to do anything else.

Kol is shirtless and glistening underneath the sun's

rays as he hauls an armload of firewood from one end of the yard to the other. His biceps flex and bulge with the strain.

My breath catches. I drink him in.

Iynx's hands land lightly on my hips and rub soft circles against the fabric of my dress. My body comes to life, tingling and zinging with rays of pleasure that pool between my thighs.

My head spins, and my knees wobble as images of Kol's body pressed to mine fill my head.

"Pleasure is about more than sex." Iynx's voice is soft in my ear, barely a whisper. Her breath on my cheek smells sweet. "It's about accepting what you feel. What you want. What you need. Embrace your desires, darling. Accept them as part of you, and they will make you stronger."

I sigh, my limbs liquidy and my thighs aching. Iynx is right. If I just give in and walk out there and offer myself—

"Whoa. Hold on." I step away, nearly wrenching my body out of Iynx's grasp as I stumble back to my chair.

"Feel it," she encourages. "Breathe through it."

The door opens, and I groan as Kol strides across the room.

"What's wrong with her?" he demands. "What happened?"

"She's fine." Iynx waves him off, but he drops to one knee in front of me.

"Elidi, what's wrong?" he asks.

"Impeccable timing," I mutter.

"What?" he asks.

"Nothing." I take one more deep breath and will the flush in my cheeks to get lost. Then I lift my head and meet Kol's eyes. "Iynx was just showing me a little of what she can do."

Kol cuts Iynx a sharp look. "Really?"

"She wants to know more about what she is," Iynx says, and her innocence is way too forced. I look up at her, but it's Kol who responds.

"What she is. Not what you are," he says.

Iynx shrugs. "It's all connected." She winks at Kol and adds, "But I don't have to remind you of that."

His jaw hardens. "Iynx," he warns, but she backs away, her hands up in defense of some unspoken offense I don't understand.

"Kidding, kidding," she says, and the teasing in her tone is replaced by solemnity. "Kol, you know I'd never hurt her. I just want her to accept all of herself. I want the same for you."

He stares back at her for a long moment. I can tell he's angry, but he doesn't argue with her or comment further about whatever it is they're both alluding to. Finally, he looks back at me.

"Are you all right?" he asks.

I nod, hating the way they've just discussed my near-orgasm like it was some sort of physical attack. Although, considering the onslaught of sensations, maybe "attack" is accurate.

"I'm fine. Just a little . . . overwhelmed," I tell him.

He presses his fingers to the pulse point on my wrist.

"What are you doing?" I ask, confused and a little wound up at his touch considering where my thoughts have been.

"Just checking on you," he says.

"But how—"

His hand moves to cup my cheek, and he peers intently into my eyes as if searching for something. I lean in, closer and closer until we're nearly nose to nose. He releases me so suddenly I have to catch myself to avoid face planting into his shoulder. I sit back, and Kol stands, putting some distance between us.

"I told you she's fine," Iynx says.

"I'm going to get her some water," is Kol's only reply.

He turns for the door, and I call to his back, "I already have lemonade."

He whirls to glare at Iynx, furious all over again.

"Tell me you didn't."

"What's in the lemonade?" I ask, eyeing my empty glass with a ball of panic in my stomach.

"It's infused with Iynx's power," Kol says.

"Wait. Are you saying you fed me some sort of sex-ade?"

Kol glares at Iynx.

"We talked about this," he says in a low voice.

Iynx takes a step forward. "Kol, now listen—"

"No more, Iynx. I mean it." His tone is harsh and biting, but Iynx only rolls her eyes, unruffled. Kol's eyes narrow.

"Promise me."

"Fine. No more lemonade," Iynx says.

Satisfied, Kol nods once then heads for the door.

The moment it shuts behind him, Iynx looks down at me and winks as she adds, "Today."

CHAPTER ELEVEN

TWO more bubble baths and one good night's sleep later, I finally feel like me again. Iynx steers clear of me, and there's no more pink lemonade. Only water and the best food I've ever eaten. Kol delivers it to my guest house on a silver tray and then retrieves it when I'm done. He doesn't say anything about my sex-ade trip, and I don't bring up our kiss.

I dress in my leggings and tunic, which are freshly washed and sitting out on the dresser when I emerge from the bathroom. Having them back feels important like I'm expected to do something today. Which is good. My impatience has become a second skin.

I scarf down the fruit and juice on the tray Kol left then wander outside in search of him.

He's in the backyard, building some sort of sculpture with tin cans and piles of firewood.

"Are we having a bonfire?" I ask.

He looks up, and his eyes do a quick scan of my body that leaves me tingling.

"Something like that," he murmurs.

"Okay, before we go any further, I think we need to establish a few ground rules."

"Like what?"

"First, no more veil jumping. I can still feel my organs moving when I walk, and it's weird."

His lips twitch. "Your organs aren't moving. It's just the vertigo."

"Vertigo is dizziness. I'm not dizzy, I just—"

I wobble, and Kol grabs my elbow, steering me back onto the path before I can veer and fall.

"Fine, I'm a little dizzy," I grumble.

Kol turns away but not before I see him smile.

I glare and wrench my arm out of his grasp. "This only proves my point."

"Okay. No more veil jumping," he says.

"Second, I get to know all the things."

"What does that even mean?"

"It means you should have told me what Iynx can do. I thought I made it clear before, but just in case, I will not follow you around like a lost puppy. You tell me what's happening and what I'm walking into, or this won't work. Deal?"

A muscle in his jaw works back and forth. Finally, he says, "Deal."

"What are we even doing out here other than hiding?"

"Training," he says, gesturing to the cans.

"You want me to compete in an eating contest involving non-perishables?"

"No, I want you to shoot them."

"Shoot them," I repeat, my confusion growing. "With what?"

"Your magic."

I cut him a look, brows raised. "I don't—"

"Like you shot me," he adds, and understanding dawns.

"That weird flash of light in my kitchen."

He nods. "It stopped me in my tracks."

"But I don't know how I did it," I argue. "Or what it was. That was the first time anything like that's ever happened."

"Today will be the second," he says, undeterred.

"And you want me to shoot hot sparks here? In the desert?" I ask. "Did our walk yesterday not teach you about the lovely effects of heat exhaustion?"

"Training in extreme temperatures makes you a better fighter."

"Like whatever doesn't kill you makes you stronger?" I ask.

He shrugs. "You're the one who told me you never sunburn. And you handled our walk here without food or water better than any human would have."

"So I'm good with heat. Doesn't mean we should tempt fate—"

He hands me a candy bar. "I noticed yesterday you seem to like these," he says.

I eye him then the chocolate dubiously.

"What?" he asks.

"I don't know if I trust it," I say. "Need I remind you of the sex-ade incident?"

"This isn't like the lemonade." He stresses the last word.

"Riiight. Didn't your mother ever tell you not to take candy from strangers?"

"I'm not a stranger," he points out. "And my mom's dead."

The way he says it, completely flat and matter-of-fact, makes me look up sharply. My heart pings with an ache of sympathy—and understanding.

"I didn't know. I'm sorry. How did she die?" I ask.

"Labor was too much for her. She died when I was two days old," he says.

"Kol, that's awful. I'm sorry."

He looks into the distance, his gaze a million miles from here. I don't say a word, letting him process whatever he needs to. But he just shakes his head.

"It's been a long time. It's not a big deal."

"Losing a parent is always a big deal," I say. "What about your dad? Where is he?"

"He died two years ago. Demon attack." His words are even more clipped than before, and I forget all about the candy bar I'm still holding.

With my free hand, I reach for him. He steps back. A moment of silence passes, and I try—and fail—to read him.

"What kind of demon?" I ask finally because I have to know. Because everything else about this new life is digestible. Wolf guardians? Sure. Gods and goddesses? Why not? Demons? I already saw the horses from hell.

"Gray skinned, hollow eyed kind with massive strength. Otherwise known as hellions. They're Hades' creations. His soldiers. They attacked my father's campsite while he was on a recon mission for Vayda."

"I thought the war ended and Hades was banished to Hell? How are the demons getting through the veil or whatever?"

"That's what the recon mission was about," he says. "Hades has never given up on his quest to rule the gods. Over the millennia, he's tried various tactics from infiltrating the human world to seducing humans into doing his work. The more chaos he can create here, the easier it is for him to send in soldier-demons unnoticed."

"So the demons can look human?" I ask.

"Some have the ability to shapeshift. It didn't used to be a threat because for a few centuries, the world was relatively stable. But a few decades back, we uncovered one of his soldiers in Germany. In fact, the creature managed to start and lead an entire human war before we were able to stop him."

"Germany?" My eyes go wide. "Are you saying Hitler was a demon?"

"I'm saying it's the closest Hades had gotten in centuries to actually causing the chaos he needs to invade again."

"That's crazy. So demons are still running around here in disguise, trying to overthrow human civilization?"

"Most often, they infiltrate politics, but the ones that can't shapeshift tend to roam in the rural areas of the world in order to hunt."

"To hunt what?" I ask.

"Gods."

I swallow hard.

"My dad was tracking a small pack of them in Canada, but he got too close." His expression darkens. "If it weren't for this ridiculous feud—"

He breaks off and fists his hands, clearly done with

this conversation.

I try to think of something to say, but I know from experience that nothing will erase a pain like that. Instead, I do the only thing I can think of that can possibly move us forward. I peel back the wrapper of the candy bar and take a huge bite.

I chew, swallow, and take another.

By the time I'm done, Kol is watching me with faint amusement.

"What?" I ask around a mouthful of granola and oats.

"I've just never seen someone take such large bites before," he says.

"I have a large mouth." The words—though muffled by the food—register too late, and I realize Kol knows it because his half-smile turns into a full blown grin.

"Trust me, I know all about your mouth," he says, and my cheeks heat at the memory of his mouth on mine.

I pretend the candy bar is too much of a mouthful to form a response.

"Ready?" he asks when I'm done.

I nod.

"Good, let's get to work."

We start with stretches, and I'm just recovered enough from the vertigo to remain upright. By the end, I'm feeling confident—even if I am already soaked in sweat.

"Get some water," Kol says, tossing me a towel.

I use it to wipe my face and neck then happily do as he asked. When I'm done, Kol's already waiting.

As I approach, he bends his knees and squats into a crouch. The moment his hands come up, my confidence plummets. The idea of fighting Kol—even for training—makes me want to rethink my plan.

"I thought you said you wanted me to practice shooting sparks from my hands," I say.

"You said yourself it's only happened once. If I remember correctly, you were trying to fight me off. I thought it might help to recreate the scene."

I bite my lip, eyeing Kol's giant muscles. If it weren't for the vertigo, I might convince myself I could take him. But the idea of it only makes me think of Finn and how he used to help me demonstrate self-defense to the women in my classes. So far, I've managed to distract myself away from the betrayal of my best friend—or the questions it raises. I can't help but wonder what secrets drove Finn to burn my house.

"Besides," Kol goes on, "physical exertion can help to trigger your ascension."

That gets my attention. "It will?"

He nods, and I shove aside thoughts of Finn and what he might know.

"What else will trigger my ascension?"

Kol hesitates which only makes me more suspicious and determined for an answer.

"Kol?" I press.

"Tell you what, you train with me now, and I'll tell you when we're done," he says.

"You're manipulating me."

"One hundred percent."

"You're not even trying to deny it?"

"Nicnevin isn't going to stop, so I'll do whatever it

takes to make sure you stay alive. You need to be ready."

"You sound like my aunt. She was always enrolling me in self-defense classes because *you never know,* and *being a pretty, young girl makes you a target.*" I do my best impression of Aerina's voice before I realize Kol's never met her.

"She sounds smart," he says.

"She is." I frown. "Or she was."

Kol steps closer. "She is," he says quietly. "Elidi."

The sound of my name makes me blink. I look up at Kol and find him studying me with concern lining his features.

"We'll find her," he says.

"I know." I nod, and my resolve slides back into place. "Fine. Train now. Information about ascension later."

"Deal," he says.

"And I get another candy bar," I add.

He rolls his eyes. "If you beat me, yes."

I smirk, but he just beckons me forward.

For the next hour, Kol and I spar.

He's strong, but I'm fast—normally. Unfortunately, my body is awkward thanks to the vertigo still plaguing me, and none of my attacks sneak past his defenses. Twice, he manages to knock me on my ass thanks to the slickness of his skin distracting me from his right hook.

By the time we break for water, I'm sweating and frustrated.

"How long did you take those classes?" he asks.

"Off and on my whole life." His brows shoot upward, and I scowl. "In my defense, those classes were for fighting off other humans. And, my organs are still jiggly. You have an unfair advantage."

He fights a smile. "Give it another day or so. It'll pass."

"Do we have that long before The Silenci find us?" I ask.

Kol doesn't answer.

"Have you heard anything from Grim or Vayda about where Aerina might be?"

"Not yet. But if anyone can find her, it's the two of them." He says it like it's not a good thing.

"Do you think Nicnevin hurt her?" I ask quietly.

"No."

His certainty surprises me, and I look up at him sharply. "How do you know?" I ask.

"Honestly, because there's no strategy in that." He grimaces. "If she wants to get to you, the best way is through your aunt."

My hope turns to fear. "You think she'll use Aerina . . . as bait?"

"You're a goddess, Elidi. You were born for more than what your mortal body is capable of. So don't give up. You'll figure out your ascension," he says. "I promise. Now, come on." He punctuates his words with a shake of my shoulders.

I blink, stepping back to regain my balance. "For a guy who didn't want this job, you make a lot of promises," I grumble.

He smirks. "Once I'm in, I'm in. And I always give one hundred percent."

I narrow my eyes. "Are you trying to say I'm not?"

He shrugs. "I'm just saying you couldn't knock me

down if I stood on one leg."

I grit my teeth and drop the water bottle at my feet. "Wanna bet?"

His eyes gleam. "I don't bet. I make promises, remember?"

My mouth tightens as I try to size him up, assess his weaknesses. "Fine, I promise that I'm going to take you down."

He lifts his chin in silent challenge. "Bring it, spitfire."

With a battle cry that Braveheart would have been proud of, I charge.

Kol's body angles right, but I've anticipated his sidestep and follow him, lining both our bodies up perfectly.

I meet him head-on, but rather than knocking him off balance, his feet remain firmly planted as my body crashes into his. Strong arms come around my waist, holding me in place where my chest presses against his. It's like slamming into a brick wall. A seriously muscled, warm, sweaty, attractive brick wall.

Kol leans in and our mouths meet in a perfectly aligned kiss before I wrench backward.

"What the—"

I wiggle, trying to escape him, but his arms are strong and fastened tightly around me.

I'm trapped.

Kol's chest and belly shake as he throws his head back and laughs out loud.

"Put me down," I growl.

He only laughs harder, and I finally realize he never expected to dodge me at all.

"You weren't supposed to catch me," I complain, still wriggling.

"What else am I supposed to do when you come at me like some kind of spider monkey?" he asks through his laughter.

"I don't know? Fall?"

Kol grins down at me. "Good idea. I'll work on that," he says. "Meanwhile, that attempt was adorable."

"Shut up." I narrow my eyes, thinking of all the many ways I want to hurt him.

He winks and strokes a hand down my sweaty back. I decide to blame the smoldering in my belly on the desert heat.

"Kol, I swear to all the gods, if you don't put me down right now," I warn.

"Whoa, kids. No need to swear at me. I have nothing to do with what's happening here— unfortunately." Grim's voice is unmistakable. And close.

I twist in Kol's arms as Kol makes a sound a lot like a growl.

"Now, now, I'm not the enemy, remember?" Grim says. "How is the training going? From the looks of it, Elidi's already very agile. I'd be happy to help test that."

Grim winks at me, and I decide that when it comes time to demonstrate my goddess powers, he's next on my list.

"Training is going great for your information," I tell him.

"Yes, I can see that," Grim says, and Kol snarls.

Grim backs away. "Okay, okay," he says, "I'm going to find Iynx and offer a pleasurable hello." I roll my eyes. "You two have fun." He heads for the house, calling over his shoulder, "But not too much fun."

Kol shoots a murderous glare at his friend's back. I do my best to match it.

CHAPTER TWELVE

SOMETHING tugs on my shoulder. I moan tiredly and open my eyes only to squint at the sudden brightness. White, hot sunlight streams through the large window beside my bed. Haloed in its beams is the form of a familiar face.

"Grim, what the hell do you want?" I complain. "It's early."

"Actually, it's nearly eleven, princess."

"Whatever. It's early somewhere." I roll over, shielding my eyes from the sun—and from Grim's way too chipper expression.

"Come on. It's time to get up." He pokes me in the ribs, and I jump, twisting to glare at him.

"Don't I get a day off?" My body feels like it met with a brick wall.

Grim's lips curl, and he sits on the bed.

"You *do* get a day off. Well, from physical training. Today, you're with me. And we have a lot to do if we're going to wake up those sleepy goddess gifts of yours. So . . ." He scoots over, making room for himself to stretch out beside me. "You can either get up and get dressed and meet me outside, or we can start right here."

He reaches for me, and I flail out of his way.

"Whoa! What the hell?"

Grim lounges against the headboard with his hands folded over his middle. His green eyes are laughing, but his expression is solemn as he says, "Apologies. No more touching without permission."

"Damn right," I grumble.

"But it did help you make up your mind." He swings his legs over the edge of the bed and stands. "See you out there then."

He winks and shuts the door behind him. I flop back onto the bed and huff up at the ceiling. For a split second, I'm tempted to climb back underneath the covers, but I have no doubt Grim will reappear if I do. And there's no telling how far he'll go to drive me out of bed next time.

The thought of that has me jumping up and hurrying to get dressed.

Grim is waiting in one of the chairs when I emerge. He doesn't look up until I'm standing before him, blocking his view of the abstract piece hanging on the opposite wall that was holding his attention.

"Do you like art?" I ask.

"I like to get lost in beautiful things," he says, and there's a heavier note to his tone that wasn't there earlier—despite the fact that he's grinning slyly at me now.

"Are you always such a flirt?" I ask, dropping into the chair opposite his.

"Only with girls who resist," he says. "It's more fun

that way."

"So if I respond to your flirting, you'll stop?"

The corner of his mouth lifts in a charming half-smile. "No, you're different from the others."

"Different how?"

"If you respond to my flirting, we'd undoubtedly move on to . . . other things."

I shake my head. "I bet your mother had her hands full with you."

His expression falls, and I realize I've stepped in something I shouldn't have. Again. "Sorry. I was just—"

"No, you're fine. My mother is Silina, the Goddess of Shade."

"What does that title mean exactly?"

"It means her power lies in trickery and manipulation. It means she's not someone you want watching your back." He sighs. "Suffice it to say we don't keep in touch."

"Grim, I'm sorry." He waves me off. "What about your dad?"

He winces a little. "My dad is a little busy for me." My brows wrinkle at that and he explains, "My father is Odin."

"Oh." My eyes go wide. "Like directly?"

His expression turns wry. "Well, there wasn't a middle man if that's what you're asking."

I roll my eyes. "You know what I mean."

"It's not as big of a deal as it sounds. Odin has hundreds of children. Which is why he doesn't really have time to keep in touch with all of us."

"You mean he wasn't part of your life growing up?" I ask.

"Not really. I see him on holidays, but those are always so crowded and chaotic, especially for me." His smile is sad and pained. "Being the God of Secrets comes with certain burdens. Crowds are not pleasant."

The God of Secrets? That sounds . . . heavy. "So, can you just read people's minds to glean whatever secrets they're keeping? How does it work?"

"It's stronger with some than others. I think it has to do with how open or closed the person is to letting others in. Or how much they have to hide. The bigger the secret, the easier it is for me to pick up on. But I don't always understand all the details. It's more of a feeling." He cocks his head and leans in. "Unless you let me touch you. Then all bets are off."

I tuck my hands behind my back and wait until he leans away again. For some reason, my heart is pounding as I ask, "And what kind of feeling do you get from me? Any secrets?"

"Sorry, I don't divulge."

"But they're my secrets."

"Doesn't matter. There's only power in *holding* secrets. Once you tell them, you've given that power away. Besides, you don't need me to tell you what you're hiding, princess. You already know."

He winks, which makes my jaw fall open a little. He's either playing me or warning me not to push him. Either way, a shudder ripples through me at the kind of power Grim's bank of secrets undoubtedly holds. I can only assume holding on to the secrets of the entire world is no small thing.

And despite his bravado and slick talk, my heart pangs in sympathy for Grim. I just hope my gifts aren't quite so heavy.

"Is that what you're wearing then?" he asks, totally jarring me.

I look down at my spandex pants and sports bra with a frown. It was the only practical choice among Iynx's mountain of gowns.

"Yeah. Why?"

"Nothing. I mean, you won't get any complaints from me, considering how well those pants show off your assets." His grin is crooked until I wipe it off his face with a sharp kick in the shin. "Ow." He uncrosses his legs and scowls. "I just meant that we won't be doing much physical exertion today. Sadly."

"Grim," I warn and he goes on, steering back to business without missing a beat.

"We'll be starting our training off by filling you in on some background about what you are and the world you come from. I thought offering some answers would go a long way toward accessing whatever gifts you have."

"Thanks, Grim. That's perfect."

He winks. "That's what they all tell me."

I roll my eyes. "I don't know how you and Kol have managed a friendship—or how you fit into doorways together, considering both of your heads are so big."

"Don't worry. We balance it out for one another with constant insults and the occasional drunken brawl."

"Well, you have one thing in common." I snort. "You're both full of it and complete asshats when it comes to dealing with other people."

Grim's gaze turns way too knowing for me, and I

shift my position, acutely aware of how easily he sees right past my flippant words into some much darker, deeper place inside my head.

"Try to cut Kol some slack, all right? He's under a lot of pressure, princess."

"We're both under pressure, Grim. I have to figure out how to ascend to save my aunt all while trying not to die at the hands of a murdering goddess. If I manage all that, I'll still be an immortal goddess in the end, and I don't even know what being that means. Kol will be able to return to whatever life he had before his oath."

Grim sighs. "You still don't get it."

"What's the big deal? He promised to protect me, and he will. I'm not saying my job will be hard—even though that's how it's looking right now—I'm just saying he'll be able to go back to what he knows when it's all over. I won't."

"His oath to protect isn't a one-time deal, Elidi. It's forever. And it's an oath sworn to Odin himself. It's not something you take back."

I stare back at him, stunned. Not only did he use my actual name—which feels serious—but one word in particular sticks out. "Did you just say forever?"

Grim arches a brow. "As a matter of fact I did, yes. Kol is your Guardian for life."

"My immortal life." I swallow hard as the sheer mathematical quantity of the word settles over me like some sort of weight.

Grim casts his eyes upward as if he's talking to some higher power as he says, "Now she's starting to get it."

"How can he just promise something like that

without asking me first? Don't I get a say in something that directly affects the rest of my life?"

"Relax. You get a say in the most important part. He will protect you forever or as long as you live, but he can't bond with you without you taking your own oath for him."

"Bond? Okay, now you're really losing me, Grim."

He drums his fingers impatiently against the armrest of his chair. "You know, I can see where the phrase 'ignorance is bliss' came from. Trying to explain all this to you just gets more and more fun."

My eyes narrow. "It's not my fault everyone lied to me. All I'm asking for is a little truth and, like, five minutes to let it sink in. Is that too much to ask?"

His irritation smooths out almost instantly. Something passes over his expression—a sort of understanding that I didn't expect and leaves me a little concerned. "No, princess," he says quietly. "It's not. I'll try to be patient with you if you do the same for me, all right?"

"All right," I say, uncertain about what made him come around so easily. Something tells me he's been in my shoes before. Lied to, maybe? But how could the God of Secrets possibly have been duped?

"Bonding is something that happens between a guardian and a god to solidify the protection. It must be consensual, and once the ceremony is completed, the bond is strengthened between the two, allowing the guardian to better protect the god or goddess."

I snort. "You make it sound like you're explaining the birds and the bees."

"The birds and the bees?" His brows knit. "I don't

understand."

"Sex, Grim. It sounds like you're explaining sex." My humor ends with Grim's strange expression. "Wait. Is it sex?"

"Sex is often a part of the equation. Not always but usually. The pairings are based on chemistry and connection. It's a divine calling and one that is always well-matched for both involved. It's very common for a god or goddess to take their guardian as a consort."

"A consort," I repeat. "As in, they get married?"

Grim shakes his head. "No. Gods and goddesses are unable to procreate with guardians. For this reason, most gods don't marry. It's more likely that they'll bond with a guardian who later becomes a consort and then also have a relationship with a god or goddess for procreation purposes."

My nose scrunches. "So, like polygamy or something?"

Grim sighs, and I can tell he's trying to reign in his patience like he promised. "I don't make the customs or rules. I am only telling you how it's been done for millennia."

"Okay, well, I'm telling you that I have no intention of taking a consort." My skin heats as I try to imagine Kol and me bonding and then consorting. "And I'm not going to have a side-piece god boyfriend either."

Grim shrugs. "Whatever you want, princess."

Silence follows, and it feels awkward, mostly because I have a sneaking suspicion we're both picturing me consorting with various gods and guardians, and it just feels so weird to be sitting here with Grim while we both imagine me naked.

I kind of want to ask Grim if he has a guardian of his own, but I suspect he doesn't, or they'd be here right now. He definitely seems like the consorting type. Instead, I clear my throat and ask, "What else is required for me to ascend?"

"First and foremost, you need to develop your gifts. We'll begin drawing them out today. How long it takes is up to you, but the process should jump start your ascension. Once your gifts begin to emerge, you will need to use them to their full capacity in order to trigger the ascension."

"That sounds easy enough."

"Not necessarily. True ascension is achieved when you can use your abilities to defy the laws of the Universe—alter nature or something to that effect. When you've fully realized yourself as stronger than the laws holding the Earth plane together, you're a goddess."

"Okay, anything else?"

"Well, not that you're interested in."

"I am interested in anything that can help me. What is it?"

"Sex with another god or your chosen guardian strengthens your gifts."

"Ugh. Never mind. I take it back."

Grim laughs, and I push to my feet, leaning down to whack him. Behind me, the door opens, and Iynx's laughter reaches me even before the sound of her footsteps.

"Saved by the bell," I grumble, backing away from Grim who has the audacity to wink at me.

"Anytime you want to finish this and strengthen

those gifts, princess, the offer stands."

I gasp. "That's not what I was about to—"

"Hello, gods and goddesses," Iynx sings. She sweeps in to stand between Grim and me with Kol trailing. He stops across the room, eyeing Grim and me suspiciously.

The heat in my cheeks feels like evidence of something, and that pisses me off since I have zero reason to feel guilty for anything.

"What's up, beautiful?" Grim asks, and Iynx practically preens at his compliment.

"I have news," she says.

"You've decided to give up the single life and finally marry me?" Grim asks.

Iynx winks. "Grim, you know you don't need a ring on my finger. We can consummate our commitment to pleasure anytime."

The heat that had just begun to dial back rushes back to my face double time. My mouth goes dry at the inviting look she gives Grim. He stares right back up at her, unblinking and intense, as if he's imagining doing just that right now.

I know I should move back or look away, but I can't do either. Pleasure zings through my belly, shooting low to my thighs. Just watching Iynx is enough to remind me of the brain-melting pleasure she can give with a single touch of a finger. Without conscious effort, I find myself leaning in. Maybe they'd let me join—

"Guys," Kol snaps.

I blink, and the spell is broken. I can't tell if I'm disappointed or relieved as I step back and offer the crazy couple plenty of personal space.

But Iynx is all business again, and I marvel at how she can switch between the two moods so easily.

"Well, I thought it was strange that all signs point to Nicnevin behind the attack on Elidi and Aerina, so I did some digging."

"And by digging she means she tried reaching out directly to Nicnevin," Kol says dryly.

I take a step toward Iynx, my adrenaline instantly pumping. "And?" I prompt. "What did she say?"

"That's the thing," Iynx says, shaking her head at me. Her gorgeous hair swings as she moves. "She didn't respond, and that's not like her."

"Probably because she's out hunting us," Grim points out.

"You don't understand. Nicki and I have a connection," she says.

Grim's expression is tense, and I wonder if he's reading into whatever it is she's not saying.

"Okay then," I say.

"I went through all the usual channels, and nothing." Her hands twist nervously, and I realize she's actually concerned. "So I decided to go check for myself."

"You went to the underworld?" I can't help the high-pitched note of panic that creeps into my words.

Iynx nods, waving off my concern. "Relax, darling. I was perfectly safe. In and out before anyone could spot me."

"How could anyone miss you?" I blurt.

Iynx's lips curve, and she pats my arm. "Thank you, darling. Very sweet. But I wasn't in this particular form."

I open my mouth to ask what other forms she can take, but Grim's impatience beats me to it.

"What'd you find?" he asks.

"Nothing," she says, and her expression turns bleak again. "That's what I'm telling you. Nicki never leaves her post unattended. Not when there are souls to sort. But the gates were crowded with souls, and Nicki was nowhere to be found."

"We have to find her," I say. "She's the only one who might know where Aerina is. Does Nicnevin have a guardian?" I ask, glancing at Kol.

His dark eyes are fastened to mine, but he doesn't answer me. I can practically see his thoughts churning away, and I know he's calculating the danger we're in now that Nicnevin is missing.

Iynx shakes her head. "Nicnevin is unbound. It's the only way she can remain bonded with The Silenci."

I shudder at the reminder of those demon stallions.

"Kol?" Grim says. "What do you think?"

"I think it's only a matter of time before we're discovered here," he says. "I won't keep putting Iynx at risk for us."

She reaches for his hand and squeezes it.

"It sounds like the best way to fix all this is for me to ascend. Grim, can you get us ready to work on those goddess-gifts you mentioned?"

"Absolutely."

CHAPTER THIRTEEN

WORKING out underneath the hot desert sun is its own torturous method of training. Kol already knows it, and it isn't long before Grim realizes it too. After that, all of my training sessions take place outside. Even Iynx's lemonade—which she sneaks into my thermos when Kol isn't looking—isn't enough to stave off the exhaustion, though it does provide a pleasurable sort of laziness after a long day of failing to produce magic.

By day three, I've stabilized somewhere between dead on my feet and dehydrated. I have no idea how, but I'm handling the long hours in the baking heat. It's weird.

"Do you think it's possible my super power is just that I can stand out in the sun for hours without dropping?" I ask Grim.

A heavy coating of sweat has already dampened his gray tee, and the swimming trunks he opted for rather than slacks are clinging to his thighs. It's not the worst view ever. Or maybe that's the lemonade talking.

"You're a light goddess," he says before reaching for his water bottle. "It's possible that means you have a higher tolerance for heat and sunlight."

"Right, but maybe it's my *only* superpower. Have you thought of that?"

He frowns. "Uh, no. Kol already told me how you zapped him the first time you met. Nice try, though. Keep going."

I huff, tossing my sticky hair out of my face. Most of it is perched high on my head in a crazy bun, but a section continues to rebel, falling free to cover one eye. It's annoying as hell, but then everything's irritating when I'm this hot and this inept at Grim's tests.

"These tests are stupid," I grumble, eyeing the pyramid of tin cans across the yard. I have zero confidence in my ability to hit them with anything resembling magic or superpowers, but Grim has revealed himself as a stubborn teacher. He's not letting up until I show some sign of power.

"These tests will tell us what you can do," he reminds me.

"You know, you're starting to sound as bossy as Kol."

Grim's mouth quirks. "I figured if I could channel him, you'd be more compliant."

"I don't listen to him any better than I listen to you."

Grim snorts. "Oh, princess, you respond in all the ways that matter."

"I—"

"How's it going out here?"

The sound of Kol's voice silences my argument. I

press my lips together and glare at Grim. He just grins back at me. My temper spikes, and rather than zap the cans, I turn my full attention to Grim and shoot daggers at him with my eyes instead.

To my shock, something sharp lances through my gut, and I double over. A flash of light goes off, blinding me, and I turn away, shutting my eyes against the brightness. When I open them again, Grim is doubled over, holding his left shoulder.

Kol stands beside him, trying to pry Grim's hand away.

"I'm fine," Grim snarls.

"Then let me see it," Kol insists.

I blink, stunned at what just happened and how quickly Kol moved to help. Iynx steps up beside me, watching the boys, a glass of chilled lemonade in her manicured hand. "Impressive," she says and sends me a sideways glance.

"What?" I shake my head. "I didn't—"

"It was an accident. It's okay," she tells me and pats my hand. It's a casual touch but sends a zing of pleasure through me that feels like reassurance. A reminder that she accepts me. Wants me. It doesn't feel sexual like the others. More affirming.

"How did I do it?" I whisper, still watching as Kol manages to coax Grim into moving his hand out of the way.

Even from here, I can see the bright red skin where a blister is already forming along his collarbone.

I gasp.

"You were angry," Iynx says, and hearing it out loud only makes me feel even guiltier than before. She squeezes my hand again, numbing the pain. "He understands," she murmurs.

I turn to her. "How do you know?"

She nods. "Go see for yourself."

I let go of her hand, wishing I could hang on to the feel of her skin even after it's gone. Across the yard, I meet Grim's gaze, but there's no trace of accusation.

"Grim, I'm so sorry," I tell him.

"Princess." He grabs my hand and pulls me in, shoving Kol aside until he's tucked me into the circle of his arms. "Don't be sorry. That was amazing."

He holds me tightly enough that I believe him, and some of my guilt eases. I take a deep breath, inhaling the mysterious scent of him. Grim is an enigma right down to the musk of his skin, an unnameable smell that makes me want to unwrap him to find out more.

Huh. Maybe the pink lemonade is messing with me for real.

"You really aren't mad?" I ask when he finally lets me go.

His eyes twinkle. "I'm tougher than a goddess ascending's temper tantrum," he says with a laugh, and I scowl.

"It wasn't—"

"Although, how about next time you want a test dummy, you shoot Kol. I'm sure if we give him five minutes, he can make you angrier than I can."

Kol glares at him, and I shove him, stepping back.

"I don't want to hurt either of you."

The weight of Kol's gaze becomes too heavy to ignore, and I look over at him to find him studying my face intently. Something about his posture suggests he's thinking about more than just the burn I've given Grim. As if he's just realized I've busted him, he reluctantly looks away then glances at Grim.

"She's right," Kol says. "Let me have a turn with her."

His voice is all-business, but something secretive passes between them, and then Grim nods.

"I'll be inside if you need me." He glances at me. "Which you won't."

I don't have time to form a reply before he strides off, taking Iynx with him.

"He likes you," Kol says flatly the moment we're alone.

I blink, a little shocked that he's being so direct. Since our first training session, no, since that first kiss, he's been closed off. Unwilling to talk about anything personal. I've kept my distance too, unable to get past the whole "consort" thing. His directness throws me off.

"I like him too," I say, and Kol's eyes flash. "As a friend."

His jaw tenses.

"Gods take partners all the time." His voice is low and hard. "It doesn't have to be love."

"What would it be then?" I ask.

"Pleasure," he says simply, and I think of Iynx. Of her easy touch.

"Is that enough?" I ask, biting back the urge to ask my real question: Whether he's ever gone to someone, to Iynx, for the kind of pleasure he's talking about right now.

"That's a question only you can answer for

yourself," he says roughly. But his expression is blank, carefully masked. I don't like the wall behind his gaze, so I step closer to him, hoping to find a way around it.

"Is it enough for you?" I ask even though I'd sworn not to go there. If he says yes, I'll—

"It's not that simple."

I frown. It's not an answer. Not really. But he's already so closed off. I know if I push, he'll just walk away.

"Grim told me about the bond," I say instead.

Something flickers behind his eyes and my breath catches.

"Does it hurt?" I ask.

"Does what hurt?"

"Protecting me without it? Without my side of the oath?"

He shakes his head. "No. It doesn't hurt." His mouth relaxes. It's not a smile, but it's no longer a pained frown either.

I tell myself it's progress. To let it end here for now.

I've just begun to turn away, headed back to my position across from the cans, when he adds, "And even if it did, the pain would be worth it."

I spend dinner in the tub, trying in vain to soothe my sore muscles before tomorrow's training. After Kol's admission about protecting me being worth any pain it causes, he clammed up again. For the rest of the afternoon, we ran drills. Most of them consisted of some evil and torturous combination of sit-ups, push-ups, and burpees.

Grim is sitting in one of the living room chairs when I emerge from the bath. His eyes do a lazy scan of my pajama-clad body, lingering until I clear my throat.

He looks up at me, the opposite of apologetic, and whistles. Without missing a beat, he says, "Princess, I know you're incredibly busy, but is there any chance you can add me to your to-do list?"

"You're incorrigible."

"You love me," he teases.

"How's your shoulder?" I ask quietly.

"Healing," he says with a shrug and crosses his legs.

"Can I see?" I ask.

He reaches up and pulls his shirt down to reveal the blistered skin where I zapped him earlier. It does look mildly better thanks to some sort of cream he's slathered over the area. But it still looks painful.

"Grim, I'm still so sorry," I say, shaking my head as the guilt washes over me anew.

"Don't," he says, grabbing my hand to stop me. "Don't feel bad. This is good. We need to know what you can do. And I don't mind the pain." He gives me a crooked smile. "You can kiss it and make it better."

I roll my eyes. "I don't want to hurt my friends, Grim. I want to control my power. Besides, if I'm a goddess of light, why am I so destructive?"

He doesn't answer, and I sink into the chair opposite him, sighing as my sore muscles settle against the soft cushions.

"Relax, princess. We'll figure it out. This is all very normal. Although, if you're worried, I wouldn't mind some personal care from you. Some sexual healing, if you know what I mean." He winks, and I tip my head back while I groan.

"Don't you ever get tired of unashamedly throwing yourself at everyone?" I ask.

Grim smiles devilishly. "Not as tired as I'm sure you are," he says. "Considering you've been running through my mind all day."

"Such a player." I shake my head. "I saw you leave Iynx, you know," I say. "And now your clothes are wrinkled, and your buttons are crooked."

He glances down, and I can see his surprise when he notices his buttons are off by one. When he looks back at me, I give him a satisfied smirk, but it's quickly wiped away by his next words.

"Are you questioning my stamina or my loyalty, princess?" He leans forward. "Because I can assure you I am good for both."

I laugh. "Everything out of your mouth is a line."

His smile softens, and he sits back again. "You're having fun, though."

Something about the way he says it gets my attention. "Is that your agenda? To make sure I'm entertained? Seems a little superficial."

"Not superficial. Safe," he says, surprising me with the note of honesty in his words.

I tilt my head, understanding dawning slowly. "You keep people at arm's length to protect yourself," I realize.

He blinks, obviously a little surprised that I read

him. And I know, thanks to his silence, that I'm right.

"What are you afraid of, Grim?" I whisper, and there's no teasing in the question. If anything, I want him to know he can trust me with the answer. Because something tells me he can't trust many people in his life.

"I—" Before he can reply, the door swings open, banging against the wall.

Kol strides in, dark eyes blazing with urgency. "We need to go," he says.

"What's wrong?" Grim is on his feet instantly, and I join him, heart racing.

"The east ward's alarm just went off. Something's out there."

"The Silenci?" Grim asks.

"I don't know yet." Kol pins me with an intense stare.

Before he can move away, I grab his wrist and hang on. He drops his arm, and my hand slides into his. The touch is a reassurance, just like Iynx's, and the pleasure that sings through me is even stronger than anything I've gotten from her.

"I'm not going to let anything happen to you." His words are so filled with conviction I can't help but believe him.

In this moment, it's not me I'm worried about.

"If something's out there, it's not getting through Iynx's border," Grim says. "And if it tries, she'll just—"

"Iynx is gone," Kol says.

"What?" I gasp. "She left?"

Kol shakes his head. "She's probably trying to take care of the threat herself, but I'm not going to stand around and let her do all the work. I won't let anything happen to her for letting us come here."

Grim nods. "What do you need?"

"Go help Iynx. Elidi and I will head west. Try to slip past unnoticed. Buy us as much lead time as you can."

"I'm on it."

Grim turns for the door. Without letting go of Kol's hand, I grab Grim's wrist and pull him back. For a moment, we stand there, each of them wrapping one of their hands tightly around my own. It feels strangely right—and an undercurrent of power ripples through me as I look back and forth between them. Grim turns to face me, his green eyes sharp and cunning.

"Be careful," I tell him, nearly pleading as panic snakes up my spine. It's only been a week since Kol and Grim crashed into my life, but already I can't bear the thought of losing either one.

He leans in and presses a cold kiss to my warm cheek. Then, without a word, he turns and leaves.

Kol tugs my hand. "We need to move," he says.

I nod, not trusting my voice. But instead of leading me out the door, Kol pulls me into his arms with enough force that my body thumps against his chest. His arms wrap around me, and he buries his face in my neck. The pleasure that rocks through is more intense than anything I've ever felt.

Too soon, Kol lets me go and sets me in front of him. His dark eyes gleam nearly black in the low light. I almost pity the enemy that faces him like this. Almost.

"You're going to stay beside me the entire time we're out there. If I shift, you're going to be ready to ride me, understand?"

For a split second, full awareness colors his resolve, and his eyes darken in an entirely different way.

"We're going to revisit my word choice later," he says, and I nod, already flushing at the mental picture his words have painted.

"Fucking Hell," he mutters.

Before I know what's coming, he scoops me into his arms and presses his mouth to mine.

It's not a soft kiss. All I can feel are his hands on my bare neck, dragging my face to his. The tips of his fingers thread into my hair, and my mouth moves frantically against his. I make a sound of desperation that I have not once heard myself make. Everything feels urgent. Like we need to leave right now. Or run right now. Or get naked right now.

"Elidi." His breath is hot against my lips. The way he says my name feels like some sort of promise.

"Kol," I manage, but it's mostly a whimper. A desperate, needy request for more.

Kol groans and kisses me harder. His lips are rough, and when his tongue darts out, plunging into my mouth, my own pleasure takes over. I slip my hands underneath his shirt, running my fingers over rippling abs. He swipes once then twice then a third time with his tongue, sending shivers through my liquidy limbs.

Then, way too soon, he breaks the kiss and steps back.

"We have to go," he says, and I can hear the reluctance in his words.

I nod and take his hand.

"I'm ready," I say, braced for whatever waits outside.

CHAPTER FOURTEEN

THE yard is empty, and I shiver as I step out into the moonlight. Kol's hand tightens around mine, my lifeline in the dark as we venture off the gravel path. The world inside the barrier is silent, and Grim is nowhere to be seen. If Grim and Iynx have gone to confront a threat, they've done so outside the barrier walls.

Jogging lightly behind Kol, we veer west toward the dark line drawn in the dirt that marks where the property line ends and the ward begins.

Up ahead, something shimmers. Kol notices, and we slow our pace. The air shifts, and Kol stops completely, inhaling deeply a moment before I see the outline of an arm in the goo.

My heart races.

I look around at our options, trying to decide which way to run when Kol snorts in annoyance.

"You have got to be fucking kidding me."

"What is it?" I ask quietly.

"Helix," he says, sounding less than thrilled.

My eyes widen as I stare at the wiggling hand and what it means. I wrench away from Kol's hold.

"We have to help him."

"Elidi, wait."

Kol tries to grab me, but I sidestep him and rush forward, plunging into the gooey mess. The jelly catches hold of my body, but unlike last time, the goo barely slows my momentum.

Helix looks back at me, his eyes pleading for help. I see the unconscious woman in his arms but can't stop. We spill out the wrong side of the wall in a tangle, and I quickly scramble off the woman and Helix.

Yellow slime clings to my tongue, and I spit, disgusted.

"Why didn't you pull me through?" Helix says, struggling to sit up.

"This is much safer, trust me," I say, thinking of Kol waiting on the other side.

Helix gently rolls his possibly-dead plus one to the side. Her skin is the color of ebony, smooth and absolutely flawless despite the fact that she doesn't quite look alive. Even in her stillness, there's something foreboding about her. Something that calls me to her even while it repels me.

She doesn't stir, and I try not to think about what he's done to her. Or why he brought her here.

"Where's the Vargar?" Helix asks, getting to his feet.

Glancing back, I see nothing but desert and blink, forgetting for a moment that everything inside is invisible to the outside.

"He's waiting in there. I think." Instead of Kol

safely on the other side, I picture him coming after me and getting stuck in the goo.

Concerned, I start for the barrier. Helix grabs my arm, stopping me.

"I've been looking for you. I thought The Silenci got to you." His voice dips, and I realize he was legitimately worried.

"Well, they didn't. I've been safe here."

"This is not safe," he says. "This is a risk and not a place you want to spend your ascension in. Trust me."

"Wait, you know Iynx?" I ask.

His eyes widen, and he drops my arm to stare at me. "Iynx lives *here*? Of course. I should have known that asshole would bring you here." He eyes me shrewdly, finally taking in my dirty pajamas and what promises to be horribly unruly hair. "Please tell me you didn't drink the lemonade."

"Have you had the lemonade?" I shoot back. "Because I really think it could help you loosen up—"

Out of the corner of my eye, something moves. I look in time to see a giant goo-covered wolf emerge with a roar. Grim's just behind him, his sharp eyes assessing the scene.

Kol launches himself at Helix, and I scramble backward to avoid being taken down too. As the pair goes tumbling, Helix shifts too. The two wolves—both impossibly large and slightly murderous looking—snap and claw and lunge at each other.

"You're both going to get us killed," I say in a harsh whisper. "Something's out here, remember?"

A pressure builds in my chest, and I recognize it as the same fiery magic I used on Grim before. With lips pressed together in concentration, I aim my palm at the sand and fire. A black ribbon of something shoots out of my hand and scorches the ground at my feet.

I frown. Probably a little too much force for what I need right now, but at least I'm gaining control of it.

Hands tucked safely at my sides, I head over to break the two idiots apart the old fashioned way.

A strong arm slips around my waist, and I'm pulled straight off my feet and hauled up against a hard chest.

"Relax, princess. You can't go over there." Grim's voice in my ear is placating—and correct.

"They're going to get us killed," I say, struggling despite Grim's wisdom. And his iron grip.

"No, they won't. Iynx is dealing with the beasts that set off the wards."

I didn't love the idea of Iynx facing them alone, but Grim didn't sound worried.

"Fine," I say. "They're going to kill each other, then."

"They won't," he says lightly.

I give up struggling and glare at him.

"How do you know?"

Grim sets me back on my feet and looks down at me, his green eyes sparkling.

"Because one is protecting you, and the other one wants to. Neither will make a kill you haven't sanctioned or ordered. Besides, it goes against the pack laws to kill another guardian unless their protected is threatened."

I tuck away the fact that Kol and Helix both essentially take their orders from me.

"What if Kol thinks Helix is threatening me just by

showing up here?"

"He won't because Helix brought us a peace offering." Grim nods at the Sleeping Barbie lying motionless at my feet.

"Who is she?" I ask.

Grim opens his mouth to answer, but a piercing cry from above cuts him off. I flinch, throwing my hands up and ducking low, defensively. I feel that same pressure in my chest a moment before Grim grabs my wrists and pulls my arms down. Ribbons of fire and black smoke shoot off into the sky, narrowly missing the large bird swooping toward us.

The winged creature lands on the ground nearby, and the moment its tiny feet touch the desert floor, there's a flash of light, and the black feathers and sharp beak transform into Iynx.

"Holy shit," I breathe. "Iynx is a bird?"

"She's called a Wryneck," Grim says quietly. "Gentle until provoked, and then . . . watch out."

I can only nod as I watch Iynx shake free of the last few feathers clinging to her skin and slightly wrinkled gown.

"Any problems?" Grim asks her.

She offers him a haughty look as she smooths her hair. "Of course not. They're all taken care of."

My mouth falls open a little at the idea that Iynx just took care of multiple Silenci beasts. I almost wish I'd seen her in action.

"You all right?" Grim asks.

"Of course. Who is—"

Iynx takes one look at the sleeping woman and throws herself to the ground beside the body. A ripple of raw power shakes the ground and shoves through me hard enough to make my bones rattle.

"Nicki," Iynx calls. Then she promptly bursts into tears, crying and pleading with the ebony-skinned woman to wake up.

I turn to Grim. "Is that really—?"

"Nicnevin," he confirms. "The Goddess of the Dead."

Fear spikes through me.

"Kol," I call out.

This time, the tawny wolf breaks away from the fight. An invisible line springs to life between us, tightening as if it's pulling him back to me when I need him.

Kol starts in my direction, and Helix does the same.

"Relax, princess," Grim says. "She's not going to hurt you."

I frown, confused.

"Is she dead?" I ask softly.

"No, I sense a pulse," Grim says. "Weak but there."

Having forgotten about Grim's arm around my waist, I jump a little when his fingers stroke my stomach.

A low growl fills the air.

"Grim, let me go," I say quietly.

Grim sighs but releases me. "The pissing contests never end around here."

I don't answer him. I watch Kol and Helix, who are both baring their teeth at Grim, and hope they don't decide to unite against the hot god. Deciding to test Grim's comment about them taking orders from me, I step toward them.

"Helix, I need you to shift back so you can talk to me about what's wrong with Nicnevin," I say sternly.

"Kol, I prefer man-chest over fur. Show me some skin."

The reaction is as instant as I'd hoped.

In a blink, Kol is human again.

"Are you all right?" he asks. "I saw Helix grab you."

Helix glowers at Kol. "I would never hurt her. Everything I've done is to protect her."

Kol steps in front of Helix, leaning toward the other man ominously.

"You are not her protector, dog."

I look over at Grim who shrugs as if to say, "Pissing contests, right?"

I roll my eyes, reach out to smack both shifters, then turn to where Iynx huddles on the ground beside the woman. Nicnevin.

"Is she all right?" I ask quietly.

Iynx looks up at me with a tear-streaked face.

"She's alive," she says. "Beyond that, I don't know. I can't figure out what's wrong." She looks past me to Helix. "Where was she?"

"I found her bound and frozen inside the Chamber of the Dead," Helix says. I grimace at the mental picture his words offer.

"Who put her there?" Iynx asks. "Who would do this?"

"I don't know, but whoever did it also stole her army," Helix says.

Relief floods me.

"The Silenci weren't following her orders, then."

"Not with her like this," Helix agrees. "They're taking orders from someone, though. I had to evade them more than once as I followed your trail here."

"Can someone do that?" Grim asks. "I mean wouldn't they have to kill her first in order to break the bond?"

"Whatever stasis she's in must be a sort of death," Kol says. "Or enough of one to break the blood bond she has with them, anyway. Whoever's behind this is free to establish dominance over The Silenci without actually killing her."

"It's a smart plan. If they'd killed her, the gods would have felt that, and we would have known immediately she wasn't behind the attacks on Elidi and Aerina."

"You have a point," Grim says.

Kol scowls, and I realize this is a dead end. If Nicnevin isn't after me, we have no idea who is. We also have to help her.

"We need to get her inside. Can you heal her?" I ask Iynx, remembering the cream she gave Grim for his shoulder.

"Maybe. I need to examine her more fully," she says. She gestures to Nicnevin. "The magic won't let her pass through the wards if she's like this, though. It won't read her power signature. She'll solidify."

I glance at Helix and see him pale. We could have accidently killed Nicnevin if I hadn't knocked them out when I did.

Iynx reaches for Nicnevin, but Grim steps up beside Iynx and crouches down. "Let me," he says gently then scoops Nicnevin easily into his arms.

"Thank you, darling. I'm a little spent just now." Iynx stays close beside him, and together they pass through the wall without a problem.

When they're gone, I turn back to Kol and Helix who are both watching me.

"I guess I'm escorting both of you," I say.

Helix takes a step toward me, but Kol steps between us.

"He's not coming inside."

"He brought us Nicnevin," I say. "And saved her life in the process."

Kol glares at Helix. "If this is a trick..."

"I don't play tricks," Helix grinds out. "Everything I do is to protect Elidi."

Kol snorts. "The only person who truly has her protection in mind is her guardian—and you're not him."

"According to the divine order, neither are you," Helix shoots back.

They're chest to chest now, both of them with hands fisted and nostrils flaring as they perform some sort of alpha-asshole staring contest.

"Ugh." I roll my eyes and wedge myself between them. "As much as I'd love to see this show of testosterone play out, it's a rerun. One we're all tired of watching, so how about we change the channel?"

"Helix, you brought Nicnevin here, and since Iynx cares deeply for her, we're grateful. But don't forget that Kol is here because I want him to be here. He's my protector until I say otherwise, and that means you have to be civil to him, or you need to leave."

"Fine. Whatever," Helix mutters.

I can feel Kol's smug smile before it forms so I elbow him.

"And Kol, Helix is our guest. He's not trying to steal me away."

Kol opens his mouth, but I hold up a hand to stop him.

"If Helix tries, you can kick him out."

I glance back and forth between them with what I hope is an "I mean business" scowl.

"And if either of you pulls any kind of shenanigans other than being civil to one another, I'll kick you both out and let Grim protect me. He takes a rather hands-on approach, but I'm sure I'll manage."

Both of them widen their eyes. "Elidi," Kol begins at the same time Helix says, "He can't—"

"Agree now, or I'll leave both your guardian asses out here." I cross my arms.

"Fine," Kol says on a resigned sigh.

I bite back my triumphant smile and turn to Helix, brows raised.

"Fine," he says, his voice harder and louder than Kol's.

I smile brightly, ignoring the fact that both of them are looking at me like they want to strangle me. Instead, I hold out an arm to each of them and turn toward the wards.

"Shall we?" I ask, feeling for the first time ever like I'm the prince saving the princess. Or princesses.

CHAPTER FIFTEEN

TWENTY minutes later, Nicnevin still hasn't stirred. Despite Iynx's various potions and whispered words, the sleeping goddess lies motionless in the center of Iynx's bed. When Iynx has exhausted her supply of oils and herbs, Grim does some sort of reading, involving laying his hands on Nicnevin's face and a heavy look of concentration on his part—but it yields nothing.

"Whatever has rendered her unconscious has also left her unresponsive," Grim says. "I can't read anything from her, including how she got this way." He shoots Iynx an apologetic look. "I'm sorry."

"No, it's all right," she says, squeezing his hand as she hovers near Nicnevin's bedside.

I watch from the doorway, caught between wanting to find a way to help and retreating to the living room to run interference between Kol and Helix. They take turns pacing and lecturing the group at large—although none of us are really listening anymore—about the dangers of interfering with god-curses. The magic inside me burns and builds as they argue.

"If curses are as dangerous as you say, why wasn't I hurt or struck unconscious?" I toss back.

Whoever was pacing—probably Kol— stops, and there's a moment of silence.

"You let her get hit with a curse?" Helix demands.

"It barely touched her before I got her out of the way," Kol snaps. "She's fine."

"Is she?" Helix challenges.

I roll my eyes, sorry that I brought it up. Grim catches my eye.

"Kol, go help Iynx in the kitchen," he snaps. "She needs to cook a syrup to use on Nicki. Helix, you can help yourself to a shower in the guest house. You smell like dead bodies."

My nose wrinkles because it's a fact I've been trying to ignore.

Kol snorts.

Helix glares.

"Helix, he's right," I tell him. "Go shower so we can be ready for whatever's next."

He glares at Grim then spins on his heel and slams the door on his way out.

"I'll sit with Nicki," I say. "Grim, can you keep an eye on Helix?"

Grim scowls but nods.

"Thank you," Iynx says, brushing a hand along my arm as she passes me. Kol follows her into the kitchen.

Grim drops a quick kiss on my temple then disappears outside.

Alone with the patient, I perch on the edge of the mattress. Nicnevin's skin is beautifully smooth, but it already looks paler than when she arrived. I wonder how long she's been this way and if we'll find a way to wake her up.

"Iynx must really think a lot of you because she's freaking out."

My hand brushes Nicnevin's. The magic inside me rushes to the surface, and a spark ignites.

I gasp at the beauty of the mini-firework as it explodes and then rains down over our joined skin. In the wake of the sparks, energy surges, and I yank my hand away, but it's too late. Whatever I've managed to call up flies out of my hand and into the sleeping woman before me.

A light flashes where my hand just touched, and her skin glows. I watch as the glowing light travels up her arm and into her chest then spreads over her body. I can see the light emanating all the way through the thin blue sheet that covers her, and I hold my breath, praying I haven't cooked her like I tried to do with Grim or Iynx's bird form.

But this feels different from the fiery ribbons. It looks different too.

The glowing ball slides up and over her face and then slowly fades away.

I let out the breath I've been holding, hoping like hell I haven't done any damage.

Her darkly-lined lids flutter then slowly blink open. A pair of striking caramel eyes meet mine. A jolt shudders through me.

Her full lips part, and she reaches for my hand.

"Thank you," she says. Her voice is deep and rich, and even though she's barely speaking above a whisper, there's a note of power that transfers between us. Her gratitude vibrates all the way through to my bones.

"You're welcome," I say, uncertain. "But I'm not sure what I did."

"You broke the binding." She blinks a few more times then looks around. When she moves to sit, I help.

"I'm sorry, I have no idea what a binding is," I tell her.

"Iynx," she murmurs eyeing the room. "We're with the Wryneck then."

I nod. "She stepped out to make you some medicine."

Nicnevin grabs my hand, holding my gaze. "You did well," she says. Then she cocks her head at me, her bronze-colored eyes flitting over me, searching. "You're the light goddess ascending."

I nod warily. "Elidi. How'd you know?"

"Your power signature is . . ." She inhales deeply and finishes with, "rejuvenating."

Relief ripples through me.

"Rejuvenating," I repeat. "You mean I healed you?"

"Of course. Is that so hard to believe for a light goddess?" She smiles, but there's an edge to her softness. "The light offers energy, life. You are a healer, among other things, I'm sure."

I shake my head. "I didn't know. I'm still learning, I guess."

She pats my hand. "Of course. In the meantime, I owe you a deep debt of gratitude for saving me."

"It was nothing," I begin, but she holds up a hand.

"It was everything," she says. "And I will owe you a favor for repayment. Tell me what it is you want most, little goddess."

"My aunt Aerina is missing, and while it's obvious you didn't take her, I could use some help getting her back."

"Aerina?" Nicnevin frowns. "The Goddess of the Morning? I haven't seen or spoken to her in a hundred years at least. I'm not sure how much help I can be."

My shoulders slump, and I look away. "I understand."

"Though I could ask The Silenci to search for her," she adds.

My eyes snap back to hers. "You don't know?" I ask.

"Know what?"

"Your army takes orders from someone else now."

Her eyes widen, and her hand reaches for her throat, her fingers brushing over her smooth collarbone. "What?" She frowns then looks down. "My bloodstone amulet. It's gone."

She looks back at me, her expression urgent now. "Do you know who did this?"

I shake my head. "I only know someone has been using The Silenci to hunt me."

Nicnevin blows out a shaky breath and closes her eyes as if concentrating.

Finally, she murmurs, "The Silenci belong to the night now. That's who came for me." Her eyes open once again, and her gaze lands firmly on me as she adds, "That is who comes for you."

"I don't understand."

But Nicnevin goes on as if talking to herself. "I will hunt them," she says, and her caramel eyes harden. "I will find them and regain their loyalty." Her tone is filled with an unspoken promise of war and death.

She throws the sheet back and swings her long legs to the floor. "I must find Iynx. She'll help me recover my strength."

Heat seeps slowly up my throat and into my face as I realize what she means. Grim wasn't lying then about sex strengthening our gifts.

I shoot to my feet, desperate to clear the room before any of that gets going.

"I'll, uh, I'll just go get her," I say and then dart toward the door.

"Elidi," Nicnevin calls, and I whirl to find her standing beside the bed, her gown brushing the floor. Her head is up, and her shoulders are back, and she's regally lethal now with her sharp, cool eyes and her terrifying beauty.

"Yeah?"

"You have death inside you," she says, and I freeze. Her words strike something in me that I can't quite identify just yet.

"What do you . . ." I trail off, not sure what I'm asking—or whether I even want to know the answer.

"Your question," she says. "I can feel your uncertainty about your gifts, and I know what it's like not to know what you have." Her expression softens— or I can see that she's attempting to soften. But her eyes still hold the threat of murder inside them. I remind myself it's not me she wants to kill.

"Your powers are unique," she goes on quietly. "Especially for a light goddess."

"Unique how?" I ask and brace myself.

"I sense darkness in you too. I sense death."

I bite my lip, pretending her words aren't legit the scariest I've ever heard, and that includes Kol telling me, "You are immortal," and my favorite bakery once telling me, "We're out of chocolate eclairs."

"Do you think it's the curse?" I ask. "The night I was attacked, I was hit with something. It didn't hurt, but it feels heavier inside me than it did before."

She nods. "Perhaps. But even if someone cursed you, that magic belongs to you now, Elidi. Own it. Embrace it."

The silence stretches, and I turn to go. Her soft words follow me out.

"What's light without a little darkness?"

CHAPTER SIXTEEN

"SHE'S awake," I say, entering the kitchen.

Iynx stops looking through cupboards and whirls to face me.

"Awake?"

"Yeah. I sort of unbound her, I guess. She sent me to find you to help her regain her strength."

Iynx beams and rushes from the room. I look at Grim who straightens from his squatted search of a lower cupboard.

"Aren't you supposed to be keeping an eye on Helix?" I ask.

"He's safely showering in the guest house. Hungry?"

I nod, gripping the counter because I am way past hungry. Despite that, I do another quick check of the room, my lips parting to form the question.

Grim answers before I can ask.

"Kol's showering back there."

I glance down the hall where he's pointing and can't help but picture a naked Kol standing underneath a stream of hot water. By the time I look back at Grim, he's smiling knowingly.

My cheeks heat, and I look away, eyeing the pasta Iynx made earlier, but Grim shakes his head.

"You need a sugar bump first, trust me."

He digs through the pantry and comes away with two candy bars—both of which I promptly eat.

"One of those was supposed to be for me, you know," Grim says. He watches me with an amused smile as I lick my fingers clean.

"Oh." I offer a guilty smile that elicits a laugh from him.

"You can owe me."

"No one told me how easily favors are traded around here," I say.

Grim's smile curls into something flirty, and I find myself leaning in. Before he can meet me, the front door opens, and Helix walks in. He's wearing a pair of sweats that look suspiciously like the ones I slept in last night, and I flush over how tight they are on him.

"What?" he demands when he catches Grim and me staring.

"Nothing." I hide a smile. "Feel better?"

Helix grunts unintelligibly just as Kol emerges from the guest bedroom off the kitchen, also freshly showered. His longer hair is still dripping at the ends, and he's shirtless—which makes me want to lick things that have nothing to do with chocolate. On second thought, keep the chocolate. There's room for both in that scenario.

Kol's gaze swings toward me. I look away but not before Grim winks at me.

"How's the patient?" Kol asks.

Right on cue, a low moan sounds from the direction of Iynx's bedroom. We all exchange a look.

Grim jumps up first. "Let's take this to the guest house, shall we?"

He leads the way, and we all silently follow him out the door and over to my own living quarters.

I note that Kol's demeanor is different now than it was before he went to shower. Stiffer. More closed off. In the short time I've known him, I'm already beginning to see that when he shuts down like this, nothing good follows.

Sure enough, the moment we're all assembled in my living room, Kol whirls on Helix, his dark eyes swirling with aggression.

"Now that we're all here and everyone's alive, I think it's about time you gave us an explanation. What the hell were you doing in the Chamber of the Dead anyway?" Kol asks, and the accusation in his voice is clear.

Helix's gaze swings to me. "I was looking for Aerina."

I blink, and my heart stutters. "You were?"

"Of course." He shrugs like it's no big deal. "She's important to you."

My insides warm, but Kol snarls.

"Not to mention, whoever took her is a threat to Elidi's safety," he says. "Just call it what it is and stop sucking up. You were trying to neutralize the threat. You were doing your job."

Helix's eyes narrow. "Can't I do both?"

Kol's reply is instant and absolute. "No."

Helix scowls, and I step forward before the tension can bring them to physical blows. Again.

"What exactly is the Chamber of the Dead?" I ask.

"It's a place for mortal souls that are awaiting transportation to the underworld," Grim explains.

"Like a waystation for dead people?" I ask. I can't help but picture zombies and mummies wandering around bumping into each other. The idea of Aerina being there makes me shiver.

"But, wait. Why would Aerina be there if she's immortal?" I ask.

"At the time, I suspected Nicnevin was behind The Silenci's attacks on you," Helix says. "And the Chamber is Nicnevin's territory."

"The Chamber of the Dead is also a sort of holding cell for trapped souls," Grim explains quietly.

"Specifically, trapped immortals," Kol adds. But he's too busy glaring at Helix to see the fear that's undoubtedly registering in my expression.

"You think she's—"

"She wasn't there," Helix says.

"That's good news, right?" I ask.

"It is," Helix assures me. "She's definitely alive. I just can't get a sense for where to look for her." He frowns like he's not used to being so stumped. "I think," he says slowly, "someone is hiding her. Maybe using some sort of loophole like they did with Nicnevin's binding."

"And we're supposed to just take your word for it?" Kol challenges.

"Not mine," Helix says pointedly.

Everyone turns to Grim, the God of Secrets.

"Is he hiding something?" Kol demands.

Grim shakes his head. "No. Though, whoever's behind this is being careful to work around all of us. They're hiding behind Nicnevin and The Silenci. And they've even managed to hide from Vayda, which is a first. This is big."

I bite my lip. "Like, on a scale of one to ten, one being 'the dog ate my homework' and ten being the 'Justin Bieber is a reptile' conspiracy, what are we talking here?"

Grim doesn't even hesitate. "Eleven." Then his brows crease, and he adds almost to himself, "Justin Bieber's reptile secret is a weight I could do without." Then, louder, he says, "Tell them what Nicnevin told you."

My eyes widen as all heads turn toward me.

"Thanks a lot, Grim," I mutter.

His lips twist. "What can I say? I'm a sucker for a secret."

I sigh. "She said something about The Silenci belonging to the night, and that's who's after me now."

Kol and Helix are both quiet. It's Grim who looks interested in solving the riddle.

"What are you thinking?" I ask Grim.

"The night," he says thoughtfully. "The night comes for you. There's some truth in those words. I just can't quite put my finger on it."

"Aren't you supposed to know all the secrets?" Helix asks, and Grim's expression hardens.

"It's not a secret. It's just the way she talks," he says in a sharp voice. "I only sense things kept from the rest of the world. Like the fact that your last chosen—"

"Don't you fucking dare," Helix says, surging forward until I step between them.

"Civil, remember?" I say. "Grim, no more oversharing."

Helix seethes but backs down at Grim's curt nod.

I can't help but wonder what Grim was about to divulge that had Helix so ready to fight.

"Look, the fact is we don't know who is after me," I say. "But we have Nicnevin now, and I think she'll help us track down The Silenci and break the blood bond with whoever stole them."

"And how long do you think that will take?" Kol asks angrily.

I blink at the sharpness in his voice, but he doesn't show any sign that he regrets his tone.

"I don't know," I say. "A few days, maybe? You're the goddess experts, not me."

"We don't have days. Not if some of The Silenci were following Helix here," he practically growls.

Helix grunts his agreement, and I'm struck by the fact that they've both finally agreed on something.

"I hate to say it," Grim says, "but this is bigger than the usual protection detail. We might need to think about reinforcements or a bigger strategy—"

"Reinforcements won't help against The Silenci," Helix says. "Not unless you have an army." His brows lift pointedly. "Which I have."

"Don't go there," Kol warns.

Helix's brows lift at Kol, but it's Grim who answers.

"Man, you need to chill out," he says to Kol, which only makes a vein in Kol's neck bulge. "You don't have to like him, but you do have to keep a clear head.

Because he's right. The only way we'll stand a chance against The Silenci is with backup."

"Finally, someone sees the truth," Helix mutters, and then more loudly, "This is why Elidi needs to come back to Tegwood with me. We don't even know the threat against her, and until we do, the only place she'll be safe is under the protection of the Eggther. If you'd just give up this stubborn idea that you've somehow been called to protect her, you'd see she's safer with us. Her rightful chosen—"

"Stop talking!" Kol's words are so loud that they rattle the artwork on the walls. "Elidi isn't going anywhere with you," he says in a low voice that's more threatening than his loud one. His fisted hands shake at his sides, and I can see evidence of his wolf emerging despite his very clear effort to contain it.

No one speaks, and the silence stretches until Kol turns to me, his dark eyes blazing with a barely contained storm.

"I need some air," he says in a strained voice that's low and deep and scraping over my nerves. "And I need you to come with me."

Need.

If he'd said it any other way.

But he said *need*, and before he's even done speaking, I'm nodding yes and then taking his hand gently in mine and letting him lead me out the door.

In the darkness, Kol continues to walk, his steps longer now. Hurried. I nearly run to keep up with him, but I don't let go of his hand. His skin is hot with temper, and I know better than to let him lose contact with me when he obviously needs something to keep him grounded. Even with my firm hold on his hand, he trembles, and his form slips a little around the edges.

He smells like an animal.

"Kol," I say gently. Because damn if I want to be the one he decides to take his temper out on. But he only turns and stares at me with something like a question in his eyes.

The moonlight reflects back to me in his darkened irises until his gaze all but glows at me.

"He's probably right," he says, his low voice pained.

My eyes go wide at that. "What?"

"Helix. That asshole is right, and he knows it. It's why I've been ready to rip off his arms from the moment he showed up. I can't protect you out here, Elidi. Not on this side of the veil. Not without some idea about who is after you or why. And not with The Silenci breathing down our necks every three steps."

Not when I haven't ascended.

He doesn't say the words, but I hear them in the empty space after he falls silent.

Something inside my chest twists. "Kol, I'm still here. I think that means you've done a pretty good job of it so far."

But he shakes his head sharply. "We've gotten lucky. But I can't predict how long that luck will last."

"What are you saying?" I ask. "You can't just leave me now. You promised—"

"I'm not leaving." He closes the distance, and instead of reaching for my hand again, his rough palm slides up and over my cheek to cup my face. His other hand grabs my hip, resting there like a weight of reassurance. A reminder I'm not alone.

His stormy eyes bore into mine like he can convince me with nothing but his stare. And he's not wrong.

"Elidi, I'm not leaving. I swear it. The oath to my people and to the gods is already done. I won't go back on it. I won't abandon you. But I want you alive, first and foremost. And that means doing things I don't like."

"What kinds of things?"

"You should go," he says, and his eyes close as if he can't stand to say the words. His forehead touches mine, and he goes still as he says, "To Tegwood. With Helix. You should go. You'll be safe there, and that's all that matters."

"What?" I pull back far enough that he drops his hand from my cheek. His eyes open, and now they're desolate. Resigned.

"I'm not leaving you," I tell him.

He shakes his head. "I don't like it either, but what am I supposed to—"

"Come with me," I say.

But his expression only hardens more. "I can't. I'm not welcome there."

"What about the veil?" I ask. "You know veil jumping makes me sick. Remember Black Peak?"

He shakes his head. "Tegwood is in the Bailiwick. It's the closest to the Earth realm, and you're stronger now. You'll be fine."

I bite my lip, knowing I'm out of excuses.

"What if there's a third option?"

The idea is crazy and sudden and probably the last

thing I'll get him to agree to, but I have to try. Especially if it means staying with Kol.

"What is it?" His tone is guarded, and his brows are creased warily.

"Finn," I say, my chest aching as I say his name. "The guy in the woods the night I left with you. He knows something. It could be important. It could help us—"

"The Eggther? No way. We can't trust him. He burned your house down."

I freeze, a cold sort of awareness washing over me so hard that I'm rocked backward on my heels.

"What did you just say?"

"I don't trust an Eggther without a chosen," Kol says through clenched teeth. Then his irritation slowly lifts, and understanding dawns. His head tilts. "You didn't know?"

I shake my head, my hands fisted, my arms trembling at my sides. "Finn is a guardian," I say quietly, but it's not a question because now that Kol's said it, too many things finally make sense. "He never told me."

"I'm sorry. I thought you knew. You said he was your friend."

"He *is* my friend," I insist though I have no idea why I'm arguing that fact with Kol. Not after what I saw through Grim's portal view. The fire. Finn's gas can. But it doesn't make sense. If Finn was my friend, why burn my house? If he was an Eggther, why let me run away with Kol to safety? Only Finn can answer those questions.

"Look, it's hard enough standing here, admitting

the best way I can protect you is to send you off into the sunset with my enemy," Kol says. "Please don't make this harder on either of us."

I grab him and hug him close.

"It's okay," I tell him when he lets me go. "I'll be okay."

Because while he might be willing to send me off into Eggther-land, I know what I need to do. I need to get some answers.

I tell Kol good night and head for my room.

When I round the corner, Grim is leaning against the door of the guest house, blocking my entry. His arms are folded across his chest, and one look at his face reminds me he's the master at ferreting out secrets. My pace slows and my thoughts race to make this work.

"What's up?" I call out, hoping my tone sounds more innocent than I feel. The darkness inside me curls inward, trying to hide itself.

Grim makes a "tsk" sound with his tongue and straightens. "I thought we were friends, princess."

"We *are* friends," I tell him.

"Then why are you leaving without saying goodbye?"

"I'm just going to bed, Grim. I'll see you in the morning."

He cocks his head, studying me with a deep frown, and I know he's trying to wade through the half-truths I'm trying to spin my thoughts around right now.

"Did he tell you his reasons?" he asks.

I sigh. "He says it's the only way I'll be safe."

"You have other ideas?"

"I plan to leave in the morning. With Helix," I say pointedly.

But Grim's eyes gleam knowingly. "You know, even without my gifts, I'd see the truth written all over you."

"I don't know what—"

"It's something you should work on if you're going to fool someone like him."

"Grim, this isn't—"

He swings in and plants a kiss on my cheek, lingering just long enough that his scent hits my nose. I breathe it in, a musk that's both mysterious and inviting, until I'm knocked off balance. His arms come out to brace my elbows, and I rock forward, wondering if it's such a bad thing to let Grim hang on to me a little longer.

Grim turns to look at me, and our noses nearly brush.

In the moonlight, his eyes are soft, and there's something easier about him now than before. Something that understands my need to run.

"This isn't a journey Kol or I can make with you, Princess." A shadow passes over his features as he adds, "We're required elsewhere, and it's an order I intend to free him from, believe me. In the meantime, take care. If anything happens to you, I'll—"

He breaks off, and concern flashes in his eyes.

"Grim." I reach for him and press my palm to his chest. It's a gesture meant to reassure, but when I feel his heart racing, my mouth goes dry.

Grim is handsome in an unpredictable sort of way, and while he has an edge that makes it hard to resist his ridiculous pick-up lines and silly jokes, tonight is different. Tonight, he's confessing . . . I don't know what, but it's not as simple as friendship. Not anymore.

Grim's gaze drops to my mouth, and he leans slowly toward me.

I go completely still, waiting with anticipation.

Grim's lips brush mine softly, and I shudder with pleasure. His touch is light and feather-soft as if he's being careful. It makes me want to show him just how tough I really am. It makes me want to jump him and hang on and not let go.

Instead of deepening the kiss, Grim hovers there, waiting. Asking.

I hesitate, wondering what it would be like to kiss him back, but as much as I want to know, I don't move. Already, this moment feels like a secret. Because no matter how attracted I am to Grim, it won't erase how I feel about Kol.

"Grim," I say before his lips can touch mine again.

The light in Grim's eyes dies a little. He eases back. "I know," he says roughly.

Something about his tone makes me want to explain. "I want to," I tell him. "I just—"

"I know," he says again. He moves to walk around me then stops and turns back. "He's not rejecting you," he says roughly. "He's bound elsewhere, Elidi. We both are."

"What does that mean?" I demand.

He shakes his head. "I wish I could tell you." His voice drops to a whisper, and he adds, "Be careful."

Then, he turns and walks away.

I watch him go, unsure what to think about his cryptic words. He made it sound like Kol was being forced to send me away. And I realize how little I know about their world—or their responsibilities. But it also doesn't really change my plans. I won't be sent into hiding. Not with Aerina still out there.

I won't give up on my family.

The next morning, Grim and Kol are waiting for me when I step outside.

Neither one looks remotely happy about the plan for today.

"Where are the others?" I ask.

"They're coming," Grim says.

"Here." Iynx appears from the main house and holds out a backpack.

"What's this?" I ask.

"Food. A change of clothes. Some things to help make your journey easier."

"Thank you. For everything," I tell her.

She smiles then helps me slip it over my shoulders. "You're welcome here anytime. Should you need anything, please let me know." Her arms wrap around me in a tight hug.

When she lets me go, I catch sight of Helix approaching.

"Nicki's asking for you," he tells Iynx.

"Go," I tell her.

"Be safe," she calls before hurrying back to the house.

"You ready?" Helix asks.

I nod, but instead of following him to the border wall, I turn to face Grim and Kol. My heart aches, but I keep my expression neutral as I march up to them both and hug them one at a time. When I step back to face them, Grim wears a distant expression. Kol's gaze, however, is unwavering and piercing as he looks back at me.

"Be careful," Kol says. His voice is low and strained.

"Don't trust anyone," Grim adds.

I nod. "I'll see you both soon."

Kol's gaze flicks to Helix. "If anything happens to her," he begins.

"It won't," Helix assures him. "I'll keep her safe."

Kol doesn't answer. He and Grim turn to go.

"Wait five minutes," Kol tells me. "If we're not back to warn you, that means it's clear."

Grim grabs his shoulder, and they disappear into the goo.

Helix steps up beside me. He has a bag of his own strapped to his back; another gift from Iynx. I concentrate on calculating our supplies while we wait for Kol and Grim to scout the way ahead.

Five minutes later, they haven't returned.

"It's time," Helix says.

He offers his hand, and with a firm grip on each other, we walk slowly through the gooey wall and then out the other side.

CHAPTER SEVENTEEN

THE air feels exactly the same, and the landscape is still clearly desert, but it feels different. A strangeness that comes from exposing myself to danger without Kol or Grim beside me. But it's also invigorating to be on the move again. To be doing something productive that will, hopefully, take me closer to finding Aerina. And answers.

A bolt of energy surges through me.

I look over at Helix. He's spitting and doing his best to wipe off the goo that coats his clothes and hair. I do the same then reach into the bag Iynx gave me and pull out two cinnamon rolls, offering one to Helix.

"For the taste in your mouth," I say before taking a huge bite of mine.

Helix takes an equally large bite, and we start walking.

"What?" I ask when I catch him looking at me.

"I have to admit I was surprised when you agreed to come with me."

I shrug. "It was the best option," I say around a

mouthful of the sugary dough.

His brows rise. "Did that option have anything to do with cinnamon rolls?"

"It doesn't hurt." We walk a few paces then I add, "Also, we're not going to Tegwood."

Helix stops and stares at me, eyes narrowed. "What do you mean we're not going to Tegwood?"

"We're going to see my friend, Finn," I tell him then start walking again. Partly because the threat of Silenci drives me—and partly because Helix is looking at me like he's about to explode.

"That's not the plan," he says, catching up easily with his longer strides.

"It's *my* plan. And last I checked, guardians take their orders from their chosen."

He growls. "That's assuming your orders aren't completely stupid ideas designed to get us both killed."

"Look, I'm not going to run away and hide out while my aunt is in danger," I tell him.

"If you can't condone this, I'll understand. You can return to Tegwood, no harm done."

His eyes widen, and he grabs my arm, pulling me to a stop. "Actually, there would be lots of harm. Probably even attempted murder. Because Kol Valco will definitely try to kill me if I abandon you out here."

I don't argue. I can't. Not when he's right.

Finally, he sighs, but it's more of a resigned groan. "What does this Finn offer, anyway?"

"Information," I say.

"About what?"

I shrug. "That's what we need to find out."

"Didn't this guy burn your house down?" he asks.

"Yes, but I'm sure he had a good reason."

"How sure?" he asks, eyes narrowing.

"Almost sure." What I lack in certainty, I make up for in confidence—or at least that's what I'm hoping as he stares back at me, contemplating.

Finally, he starts walking again.

I hurry to catch up. "Does this mean you'll come with me?"

He glances at me sideways. "I'm not going to leave you out here alone."

"I can take care of—"

"Don't say it."

I frown.

For a few minutes, we walk in silence.

"What are you thinking?" I ask.

He glances over, and I wince at his expression.

"I'm trying to figure out what I did to anger the gods so badly."

I decide not to speculate for him.

By the time we reach the familiar dirt road Kol and I traveled in on, the sun is high in the sky, and my stomach is grumbling. I stop for water and then unwrap another cinnamon roll before we continue onward.

I offer part of it to Helix, but he shakes his head. "How can you eat more of that junk in this heat?"

I flash him a smile. "I need to keep my strength up, right?"

Helix watches as I eat the rest of the roll in one final, huge bite. "They say the way to a man's heart is through his stomach. Maybe it's true for you too," he says.

"Nah. The way to a man's heart is through his fourth and fifth rib," I counter.

"Where did you hear that?"

"My aunt Aerina. You do not want to mess with her." My voice catches as I remember someone already has messed with her. "When we find her, I mean. When we take care of whoever's already messing with her . . ." I trail off when I realize my attempts to fix it are only making it worse.

Helix's hand finds mine. His fingers are sticky from the cinnamon roll, but I don't mind. He squeezes once then says, "We'll find her. Together."

For some reason, I believe him.

We're just beginning to descend toward the trees on the backside of the mountain when something howls in the distance.

I look at Helix but don't stop walking.

"Please tell me that was a friend of yours," I say, edging close to him.

Helix doesn't answer except to stare in the direction of the howl.

"Helix," I whisper when he remains quiet.

"I'm listening," he says, shushing me.

"And? Do you hear anything?"

"Not with you talking."

"Fine." I glare at him then do the only thing I'm positive will shut me up and help calm me down. I eat another cinnamon roll.

Helix gives me a look but says nothing.

"Here," I say, handing the bag over to Helix. "I need to be stopped."

He takes it just as another howl sounds.

"Okay, that cannot be coincidence." Helix stops and grabs my arm.

He's staring hard at the line of trees across the road, his forehead creased in concentration.

"Helix?" I say.

"Where does Finn live?" he asks sharply. His gaze cuts from me to the woods.

"Bridgeport, Washington."

"We're going to have to veil jump to get there."

"The veil makes me sick."

"Those howls you hear are from my pack. Probably just Eggther guardians scouting. But if they catch our scent, they'll be here in minutes. If they find us, they'll insist that you come back to Tegwood. And I won't be able to stop them."

"Okay," I say, blowing out a deep breath and silently apologizing in advance to my internal organs. "Let's veil jump to Washington."

Helix tugs me straight into the trees that line the road. I hurry to keep pace since he still has my arm in a firm grip.

"You should know I don't do well with veil jumping," I warn while we crash through the brush toward some unseen destination. "So if you could just warn me before we head in there, I think—"

I feel the tingling begin a split second before I'm swallowed up and sent through a wormhole that immediately turns my insides to mush. My stomach rolls, and by the time we step out the other side, I'm already bending over and heaving up the cinnamon rolls.

Helix stands beside me, still silent. I don't know

whether to be grateful for his protective presence or mortified at his front row seat.

I straighten and accept the flask of water Helix offers. Shivering lightly in my jacket, I rinse my mouth as I look around. We're surrounded by large trees, their branches dusted in fresh snow. That explains the frigid temperature and the pine-scented air.

I hand the water back to Helix.

"How close are we?" I ask.

"The veil portal for Bridgeport is about ten miles from town."

"That's handy," I say. "Are there veil portals near every town?"

"No. A portal near a town this small is rare. You can conjure one, of course, if you're an ascended god though it won't last more than a few seconds. Most guardians and ascending live in larger cities where a permanent portal already exists. Those are much harder to create."

"So Aerina must have chosen this place for us because there was a portal nearby," I say.

"Or she's the one who put it here."

"She can do that?" I ask.

He shrugs. "I have no idea what she can do."

I duck my head. "That makes two of us."

Our boots crunch over the fresh snow as we make our way toward town. My brain swims with fatigue thanks to the veil jump. It's not quite as deteriorating as the first time, but it's still taking a toll. Beside me, Helix is sure-footed and silent once again.

I glance over at his expression, but it's all-business. I should be grateful for his singular focus on our mission. It's that kind of concentration that could save my life.

The exhaustion begins to weigh heavily.

My eyes catch on the dark, inked lines of a tattoo peeking out from underneath his collar.

"What's the tattoo for?"

He glances over, frowning. For a second, I think he's not going to answer.

"It's the mark of a protector bond," he says stiffly.

"I thought the oath was more of a verbal commitment."

"It's true. The oath is something a guardian offers to the gods. The bond is something personal between a guardian and his chosen. Their tattoos, or marks, create a magical link, strengthening their connection."

"I thought guardians could only protect one god or goddess," I say. "That it's a bond for life."

"It is," he says, looking away.

"Oh," I say, understanding.

Helix had protected someone before me, and I can't help but wonder how his chosen had died. But more than that, given his reaction, I wonder why he would want to protect another.

The sky is lightening a little as we near town thanks to the haze of light pollution. It's a welcome sight that chases away some of my unease at walking in the too-quiet forest at the cusp of dawn. I burrow deeper into the meager warmth of my jacket and glance at Helix again.

"I think I misjudged you," I say.

"What do you mean?" Helix asks.

"When you showed up at Black Peak to find me,

breaking their rules about trespassing, I thought you were some kind of rebel. And even now, you're running away with me and taking me someplace opposite of what you think will keep me safe. But you're not really a rule breaker, are you?"

"No."

I snort because his single-word answer says it all, but then I think about what his rule-breaking got him back at Black Peak, and I feel instantly guilty.

"Helix, I'm sorry. About what Vayda did to you that night."

He looks over at me, and his gaze softens.

"It's not your fault. Besides, I knew what would happen when I decided to go."

"Why'd you do it then? Why come after me at all?"

He shrugs. "When the spirits call, you listen."

"It's that simple for you, isn't it," I say because I can see that it is. If it weren't for that call, he would have gladly stayed back and let Kol handle this. "Duty comes first."

"Duty is everything," he says simply. "It's why we were created."

"And what about love?" I ask.

He frowns, and I know I've hit a nerve.

"Love is a luxury," he says quietly. "One I can no longer afford."

My chest tightens at the way he says it, and I think of his previous chosen. Rather than push him to talk, I slide my hand into his and squeeze. Or I try to squeeze though I'm not sure it works since I can't feel my hands anymore.

Helix glances over with a frown. "You're cold," he

says.

"A little," I say. Then I realize how warm his hand is in mine. "How are you not cold?"

He lets go of my hand and wraps me in a hug. Warmth emanates from his body.

"It's a wolf thing," he says, and I snuggle in closer, tucking my frozen nose up against his throat.

He sucks in a hissing breath.

"Not sorry," I say, burrowing closer, desperate for warmth.

He chuckles and rubs his warm hands up and down my back. Finally, Helix eases back to press his warm palms against my chilled cheeks. His emerald eyes study mine, and he looks a little less tortured than before. I purposely keep my eyes off his tattoo.

"Town's not much farther. Come on," he says, grabbing my hand and pulling me along.

I don't argue. In fact, keeping up with his longer strides helps keep the numbness in my fingers and toes at bay until we finally reach the outer edges of downtown Bridgeport.

From here, it's a short walk to Finn's house. Finn's porch light is on when we arrive, and something tight inside my chest loosens at the sight.

"I hope he's here," I murmur, aching for a hot shower and warm clothes. But most of all, some answers.

Helix sniffs the air then cuts me a strange look.

"Finn's a guardian?"

"Apparently," I say. "You can scent him or something?"

But Helix looks past me toward the house.

"I don't like this. We shouldn't be here," he says, his voice turning to a growl as he glares at the front door.

"You don't have to like it. You just have to be civil. We're here for a reason."

He nods, and the feral look creeping into his eyes dials back.

"Let's talk to your friend," he says, but there's no mistaking the suspicion in his words.

I sigh then turn back to the house and march up to the front door and knock. There's movement inside then the door swings open, and Finn stands there, looking tired but exactly like the friend I remember. His eyes go wide, and his mouth falls open.

"El," he breathes. Finn's expression goes from shock to anger to suspicion and settles on something I can't quite read. Then his gaze snags on Helix behind me.

"What's going on?" he asks, and I know without a doubt he knows what Helix is.

"Hello, Finn," I say. "I think it's time we talk."

He tears his gaze from Helix and looks down at me. I see the guardian in him as he meets my gaze.

He moves aside, and I step into the house, crossing over the familiar, worn hardwood until I've reached the fireplace. I stretch out my hands, letting the heat thaw my fingers and toes as Helix enters, and Finn closes the door.

When I turn to Finn, I see the old Finn for a moment. The one who worried about me and had my back.

He crosses the room, and I let him fold me into a

hug. For warmth, I tell myself. Not because I missed him.

Over Finn's shoulder, I glance at Helix who waits by the door like a bouncer, expression carefully blank as he pretends not to notice us. Helix is nothing like Kol—who would be ready to break Finn's legs for hugging me. Broken legs aside, the thought kind of makes me wish Kol were here.

Finn pulls back, studying me as he holds me at arms' length.

"Where have you been? I've been looking for you for days. I thought The Silenci had gotten you," he admits.

"Not for lack of trying," I say.

His gaze slides over to Helix then back to me.

"Have you joined the Eggther then?" he asks, and it's the casual way he tosses out the name that sets me off.

"No, I haven't joined anyone, Finn. Mostly because I have no idea who any of them are. But you do. You knew what The Silenci were the night I was first attacked. And even before that—you've known all along what I am."

My hurt and anger heat my cheeks, and he drops his hands and steps back under the weight of my stare.

"El, I'm not sure—"

"Don't," I snap, leaning in to stab him with my finger. "You've been lying to me since the day we met. I want to know why, or I'm leaving right now."

"But you just got here," Finn protests.

"And I can leave just as quickly." It's not a bluff. If Finn doesn't start sharing some honesty, I'll walk out.

The problem is I have nowhere left to go. But he doesn't have to know that.

He sighs. "Okay, fine. Look, you're right. I've kept some things from you, but it was only to protect you. That was my job. It's why I came here to live in the first place. Aerina made me swear I wouldn't tell you anything."

My heart leaps. "Aerina? She knew about you?"

"She's the one who asked me to come," he admits. "After your mom died, Aerina knew you were both in danger," he says quietly. "Aerina found me and asked me to come live here and befriend you in order to help keep you safe from the people who had killed your mother."

"In danger from who?" I ask. "If you know anything about who might have taken Aerina, you have to tell me."

His expression turns pained.

"I wish I could give you all the right answers and fix this for you. I hated seeing you taken from your home, grieving for your aunt. I've only ever wanted to protect you."

"Am I your chosen? Because the Eggther don't protect unless they're divinely instructed to."

"Sometimes," he agrees. "But Aerina saved my mother's life once. I owed her for that."

"So our friendship was a lie then?"

"No. Sure, there were things I couldn't tell you, but I care about you, El. How I feel isn't because of a favor to Aerina, and it's not a lie."

I suddenly wish Grim was here. While I believe Finn, I wonder what other secrets he might be keeping from me because my aunt asked him to.

"And how did keeping all those secrets really work out for us?"

"Horrible," Finn admits.

He reaches for my hand, and I let him.

"I'm sorry, El. Truly. I never meant for Aerina to get hurt, and I never meant to put you in danger. You have to understand . . . I'm a guardian." His gaze flicks from Helix back to me again. "I'm sure by now you realize what that means. I was following orders. I couldn't break the promise I'd made to Aerina."

"But after she was taken, you could have told me then. I thought I was seeing things."

"The police were already there when I arrived that night. Then Social Services took you away. I was going to tell you the night I came for you. But then, The Silenci attacked and you ran and—I've done nothing but search for you since the moment you left."

"You could have come with me," I say.

"I couldn't," he says quietly. "You left with a Vargar. He was taking you to Black Peak. I can't go there." His brows dip in confusion. "Speaking of which, how did you leave with a Vargar and return with an Eggther?"

I glance at Helix and slowly withdraw my hand from Finn's.

"It's a long story. One we don't have time for. I came to you because I thought you could help me. I need to know who is controlling The Silenci and where I can find them."

"What?" Finn's eyes widen. "Are you crazy?" He looks from me to Helix. "Is this what the Eggther do now? Encourage their chosen into reckless choices?"

"Of course not," Helix says, his temper brewing behind his emerald ice.

"It's not up to him," I snap at Finn. "It's my decision. And I'm not going to sit around and wait to be hunted. Not while Aerina is out there and in danger. Now, will you help me or not?"

"El, you need to go into hiding. Somewhere safe where you can train until you can ascend. Until then, you're too vulnerable." His tone is gentle but placating like he's trying to talk sense into a small child.

"Is that why you burned my house down?" I ask. "To keep me safe?"

Finn blinks. "How do you know—"

"It doesn't matter how," I say.

"There was a magical signature in that house that led back to Aerina. To you. I couldn't let just anyone find it. Not while you're being hunted. You can't leave a trail. You need to lay low. You're welcome to spend the day here. You look like you could use some rest. Crash in the guest room?"

I'm still tired from the veil jump and could use the sleep but shoot a questioning look at Helix.

"I'll keep watch," he says simply, and I offer a grateful smile.

"Thanks," I tell him.

Finn looks hurt. "So, you have chosen a guardian then."

"What? No." I shake my head then stifle a yawn. "Not officially. Helix is just helping me out."

Finn gives me a strange look, and I know he's confused, but there's also relief there.

I yawn, and Finn stands offering his hand. Before I can take it, Helix is there, pulling me to my feet. Finn narrows his eyes at Helix but says nothing. He just turns and leads the way down the hall to the guest room.

"Bed's made up," Finn says, gesturing to the extra bedroom across from his own.

"Thanks," I say, turning to face Finn in the doorway.

He nods then looks at Helix. "There's a bathroom at the end of the hall. Clean towels are in the closet. I'm up for the day, so shout if you need anything."

"Will do," Helix says but makes no move to leave me alone.

After another long silence, Finn leaves. Helix steps in and closes the door.

I barely notice. I'm already pulling down the covers anticipating sliding between the warm sheets.

"Do you want me to step out so you can change?" Helix asks.

I stop and look down at my still damp pants.

"Nah." I strip out of the jeans and toss them on the floor along with my socks.

"Wake me up in an hour," I say as I crawl underneath the covers, utterly drained. "I'll stand guard next so you can sleep."

He doesn't answer, but my lids begin to drop the moment my head touches the pillow.

"Helix," I call, fighting off the tug from oblivion.

"Yeah?"

"Thank you for coming with me," I say, the words slow and slurred as I try to talk past the point of coherency.

Sleep grabs me and yanks me under as I hear Helix mumble, "For you, Goddess, it's my pleasure."

CHAPTER EIGHTEEN

HELIX shakes me awake.

"You were having a nightmare," he says quietly.

I blink, squinting against the light that sneaks through the curtains, and look up at Helix. There's worry lining his forehead and mouth.

"It's okay. I have them a lot," I say as I sit up.

Helix sits on the edge of the bed still watching me.

"You were yelling for your mother."

"That happens a lot too," I say softly.

"I'm sorry." There's sincerity and understanding in his voice.

"Who was she?" I ask before I can stop myself. "Your previous chosen. The one you lost."

Helix looks away, and I know I've lost him.

"I'm sorry. I shouldn't have brought it up. You can take the bed now if you want." I scoot to the far edge of the bed, ready to leave to give him space.

"She was Zendara, Goddess of Symphony. We were bonded for a year before— I haven't guarded anyone since she died."

"Helix, I'm so sorry."

He nods, but I can see the raw pain that lingers even after a year. Losing Zendara must have broken his heart so badly.

"I appreciate you being here," I say. "It can't be easy being called to protect someone new after what happened. Your commitment is something I admire." I stand, and Helix follows.

"It wasn't easy," he admits. "And to be completely honest, I came here to find and protect you before even taking the oath before the gods. But I want you to know that it doesn't lessen my commitment. I won't let anything happen to you, Elidi. I swear it."

"You don't have to do that, Helix," I say, but he reaches for my shoulder, stepping close as he stares intently down at me.

"You don't get it." His emerald eyes hold mine, and I can see the determination in them. The promise. "I don't care if you've chosen Kol to be your guardian. The divine sent me to you, and I take that calling seriously. So I'm not leaving you alone no matter what. I'm not walking away from this."

My heart thunders in my chest, and my sympathy for his loss becomes something else. Connection.

No matter what happens next, I won't let Kol's presence in my life push Helix out. He's part of this now too. Part of me.

"Thank you," I tell him quietly. "Your promise isn't something I take lightly. I won't abuse it."

He doesn't answer, and something about his expression makes me wonder if his last chosen *had* abused his oath somehow.

"I'm going to shower," I tell him, stepping away. "You should get some rest."

I don't wait for his answer before I slip out and head for the bathroom.

After a shower and fresh clothes—which consist of black leggings and a bright pink sports bra and one of Finn's shirts—I'm ready for another day. Well, night, considering the sun is an hour away from setting.

The veil-jump hangover is better already, and I realize I must be getting stronger. Or maybe even closer to ascension.

In the kitchen, I find Finn pouring a cup of freshly brewed Brazilian coffee. He holds a mug out for me, and I take it with a grateful smile.

"Thanks." It burns my tongue, but the caffeine hit that follows is worth it.

"You look better," he says.

I arch a brow at him. "Are you saying I looked bad this morning?"

"No comment. How do you feel about breakfast for dinner?"

"Sounds good to me."

I take a seat at the table, watching as he goes to work scrambling eggs and frying bacon. It's such a normal routine that it makes my heart ache, remembering the past mornings we've done exactly this. Usually, I'd end my morning run here, and Finn would feed me. When we were finished, he'd drop me at home on his way to work.

"Do you really consult for fitness companies for a living?" I ask. "Or is that all part of your cover?"

"Cover," Finn says after a moment.

And even though I knew it before I asked the question, hearing him admit something else he'd kept from me hurts.

"How do you make a living then?" I ask.

"The pack provides salaries for each of its members. Guardians receive a special stipend for living expenses when they're on a mission or protecting a chosen."

"And this is an official guardian mission?" I ask.

He glances back again, confusion marring his usually smooth features. "Of course. I told you that last night. I came here to help watch out for you."

"Right, but that was a favor to Aerina. You didn't actually have a vision or calling or whatever to guard me. Right?"

He scrapes eggs from the pan to a plate and sets it down in front of me along with a piece of toast.

"There are all different kinds of guardian assignments. Not all of them are divinely inspired. Some are more practical."

Finn serves up his own eggs then joins me at the table. For a moment, we eat together in silence.

"If Aerina is gone, and she's the one who tasked you with this assignment, why remain here to protect me?" I ask. "If you're not taking orders from her anymore then who?"

Finn looks up from his own plate. "I'm here because I care what happens to you, El." He must see doubt in my eyes because he adds, "I wish we could go back to the way things were before."

"I don't know about that. I mean, having Aerina here safe, yes. But the rest of it? I think I'm better off knowing who I am and what I'm becoming."

"I should have told you," he says. "If I could do it over, I would—"

Someone shuffles in behind me, and Finn falls silent. I turn to find Helix rubbing a towel over his hair.

"You're supposed to be sleeping," I say.

"I'm fine." But he eyes my coffee then makes his way to the pot.

"There's eggs on the counter," Finn says. "And bacon."

"Any word?" Helix asks after a quick sip of the coffee he's poured for himself.

I look at Finn questioningly.

"I made some calls," he says, but the hesitancy in his voice puts me on edge.

"Calls? To who? What did you find out?"

"A couple of things," he says slowly, and something about his tone makes me brace for whatever's next.

"Like what?" I press.

"First of all, Nicnevin, the known leader of The Silenci, has surfaced."

That was no surprise to me, but how could Finn possibly know? I glance at Helix who frowns around his mouthful of food.

"Where?" he asks.

"Not sure, but she's been taken into custody by Kol," Finn says. Apparently, she's been delivered to Vayda for questioning."

The last part shocks me. Why would Kol take her there?

"The Vargar have no right—" Helix begins, but I cut him off.

"What sort of questioning?" I demand.

"The Vargar have someone whose gifts include interrogation," Finn says. "They'll use him to ferret out her lies, and they'll uncover why she unleashed her army against you." He glances from me to Helix. "It's why the Eggther allowed Vayda to get ahold of her. They know she'll get answers about why she sent The Silenci after you."

I sit in silence as the pieces click together.

Grim. He is the interrogator. A master at uncovering secrets and lies. And he and Kol have taken Nicnevin to Vayda. But why?

My frustration builds. Everyone is keeping secrets, and it's pissing me off. For the first time since discovering I could do impossible things, I want to let the black ribbons of fire out to play.

"El," Finn calls, and I blink, snapping my head in his direction so suddenly he pauses. "Are you all right?"

"What else did you find out?" I ask Finn, ignoring his question. "Anything about Aerina?"

He watches me warily. "I'm still waiting to hear back," he says.

"We don't have a lot of time," Helix warns, echoing my own impatience.

"My contacts are doing their best," Finn snaps. "If you think you can do any better—"

"Stop it." I hold up a hand, and they both shut up though neither of them stop glaring. "Finn, Helix is right. Whether you've heard back or not, we're leaving. The longer we stay here, the more danger you're in."

"Even if Nicnevin wasn't in Vayda's custody, I still wouldn't care about the danger to me," Finn scoffs.

I blink, confused until I realize he must think Nicnevin's been behind The Silenci's attacks all along. For some reason, I decide not to correct him.

"Well, I do." I stand. "I care what happens to you, which is a real pain in the ass, you know that? Even after you lied to me about who both of us really are, I don't want to see you get hurt." I stab a finger against his shoulder, adding, "You might not deserve it right now, but you're my family, Finn. Don't forget that."

He nods. "All right. I'm sorry, El, I should have—"

"Don't," I say, shaking my head and backing away. "Just no more lies, okay?"

"Okay," he says quietly. He stands and heads for the door. "I'm going to follow up with my contacts again before you go."

Helix turns and refills his cup, his shoulders rigid.

"Why would Kol and Grim take Nicki there?" I ask quietly. "It makes no sense."

"Grim told me that he and Kol had orders from Vayda they couldn't refuse. He said he would get back as soon as he could. That's all he told me, I swear it to the gods."

Kol's insistence I leave with Helix...Grim's quick agreement...So many secrets. So many lies.

A weight shifts inside of me.

"Everyone has lied to me," I whisper. "Even Aerina. Not a single person in my life has told me the truth about me. About them. I can't handle anymore betrayal."

Helix meets my gaze.

"I understand." He looks at the door, indecision on his face.

"What?"

When he doesn't answer, I lose my patience.

"Helix, just tell me. I need someone to be honest with me right now. Please."

His green eyes harden. "It's Finn. I know you two have a history, but I know how to read people. The Eggther, especially. We're trained to be loyal and honest. It's not only required if we're going to build trust with our chosen, it's a code. An honor system amongst each other. So I know how to read our kind, and I can tell you that he's hiding something. I just don't know what it is."

I sigh, nodding sadly. "I don't think you're wrong."

"You didn't tell him about Nicki being innocent," Helix says, approval in his eyes. "Why not?"

"Two can play at this game," I say.

Helix follows me out of the kitchen to the living room. Finn has switched the lights on. It comforts me against the growing dark outside.

He looks up from his pacing. At the sight of us both, he slides his phone away but not before I notice an open text screen.

"El, before anything else happens," Finn says, "I just want you to know that I really do consider you my family." Something about this tone sets off warning bells.

"Why are you saying this? What's going on?"

"Everything I've done is for your own good," he says. "You won't see that now, but eventually you'll—"

Hooves suddenly clatter on the roof above us, scraping over the shingles like thunder.

"Shit," Helix whispers. "They've found us."

Outside, something throws itself against the front door. The walls shake, and the demonic scream that follows strikes a chord deep inside me. A picture falls off the walls, and the glass shatters when it hits the dining room floor.

I turn to Finn in horror. He's pale and looking at the roof in confusion.

"What the hell," he breathes.

"What did you do?" I demand.

"El, I'm sorry. I didn't know," Finn says, anguished.

Outside, a voice rises over the wail of The Silenci.

"Elidi!"

I freeze at the sound of my aunt calling my name. There's no mistaking that Finn's not nearly as surprised by the familiar voice.

"Elidi!"

I nearly trip over the couch to get to the window. Helix's arm wraps around my waist, preventing me from getting too close.

"Aerina!" I call when I see my aunt standing in the yard.

Her clothes are torn and wrinkled in several places, and there's a cut above her left eye. Flanked on both sides by demon-horses, she's walking slowly toward the door with a clear limp.

My breath catches, and I have to bite back the sob that clogs my throat.

"She's alive," I breathe.

"What the fuck?" Finn says as he stares in horror at Aerina.

I try to move to the front door, but Helix holds me.

"Elidi, you can't," he says softly against my ear. "The Silenci want this. They're using her as bait."

My skin heats as my temper flares. The magic inside me surges to the surface.

"What am I supposed to do, then? Stand here and watch her disappear again?"

"Elidi," Aerina calls again.

I stare at her through the glass. Her features are pulled tight as if she's in pain. She glances up at something or someone I can't see.

"Don't come out," she yells suddenly before she crumples with a scream.

A swirl of darkness washes over her, clinging to her body like a shadow. My heart lurches into my throat as she remains still, and the cloud thickens, spreading over the yard like a midnight fog. Within seconds, Aerina is lost inside the murkiness.

I scramble out of Helix's hold, but he pulls me back.

"You can't go out there," he says again, fighting to keep me from the door. "It's a trap."

"I have to, Helix. Someone's hurting her."

I slam my palm against his chest, and Helix flies backward, crashing into the wall. He sits up, dazed, and a patch of black energy stains his skin where my palm landed.

"Shit," he mutters.

I can't even bring myself to apologize. Instead, I scramble for the latch and slide it back.

I barely twist the knob when strong arms lift me off the floor, and I'm carried across the room. I'm seconds from sending Finn across the room too when he places me on my feet again near the fireplace.

"El, I didn't know. I didn't realize. I'm such an idiot." He's breathing heavily, and his expression is desperate now. "I thought it was a separate incident, an outside threat, but it wasn't. Helix is right. It's a trap. You can't go out there."

A fist plows into the side of his face. I whirl to see Helix staring down at a crumpling Finn with a satisfied gleam. Finn moans from where he's crouched on the floor.

"What the fuck," Finn sputters.

"Don't ever touch her again," Helix warns.

"We have bigger things to worry about," I say.

"You're right. I'll lead The Silenci away," Helix says. "Then you can run. Take Aerina. Find the portal."

"Helix, they'll kill you if you go out there alone."

"Not before I lead them away." He shakes his head once. "I can't let them have you. I won't fail again."

"Helix." I'm struck silent. It's not just the words he's saying but the casual way he's said them. Like dying for me is no sacrifice at all if it means keeping me safe.

"No one's sacrificing themselves for me ever again," I say. "Finn, tell them I'll make a deal."

"What?" He blinks.

"What kind of deal?" Helix asks.

"Tell them I'll surrender if they let Aerina go."

"No way," Finn says at the same time Helix growls, "Hell no."

"Now you guys want to agree on something?"

"El, you can't do that," Finn says. "She'll kill you."

"Who will? Who is *she*?"

Something hard hits the front window, and the glass shatters inward. I scream and duck, covering my face with my hands. Helix grabs me, tucking me in against his chest. Finn crowds in too, shielding me with his body.

I wait for the sound of the howling to start up again, but everything has gone silent. When I straighten and push the guys away, I see a woman standing in the living room, brushing off shards of glass like they're mothballs.

Her eyes gleam pure black in the light of day, and the midnight fog curls in around her, cuddling up to her like a cozy blanket. Her hair, onyx and straight as a razorblade, hangs to her waist, and there's something sensual yet dangerously terrifying about the pinprick of light gleaming from the center of her crazed irises. Everything about her screams of power.

"Hello, Elidi. I've been looking for you for a long time." Her voice is low and rough, and the sound of it makes my skin crawl.

"Who are you?"

"My name is Nyx," she says.

"You're a goddess." It's not even a question considering the sheer power clinging to her.

But she nods. "I am the Goddess of Night. And I've come to let the darkness swallow you whole."

CHAPTER NINETEEN

HELIX is the first to move. He shoves away from me, shifting from human to wolf. His dark gray fur stands on end, and he unleashes a growl as he leaps at the night goddess. She raises her hand, and a wall of fog pours from her open palm. Helix is swallowed by the dark cloud, and there's a thump as he's driven sideways and into the wall. He grunts when he falls and hits the floor.

For a moment, I can only stare, dumbfounded, at a power that looks a hell of a lot like my own fiery ribbons.

"I brought your aunt home, and this is the thanks I get?" Nyx snaps. "You sick your dogs on me?"

"You brought her here to get to me."

"I brought her here to show you what awaits you." There's malice in her tone that I don't understand.

"What the hell did I ever do to you?" I demand.

"Ask your friend," she says and raises her hand, pointing her palm at Finn as she steps closer.

I jump in front of Finn, lifting my hands, and

summon whatever power I possess. Nothing happens beyond a hot flash that warms my skin until I'm sweating and breathless. I grunt in frustration and fist my hands, ready to fight with what I have. Behind her, Helix has nearly torn free from the fog and is inching closer to Nyx.

"What do you want?" I ask to buy time.

She smiles, and it's both beautiful and terrifying.

"You, of course."

She sprays more fog, and this time I know it's for me. It hits me like a wall of ice, and I'm driven back against the brick fireplace with a grunt.

"Elidi!" Finn yells.

The fog encircling my face is too dense to see through. I'm blind to what's happening.

From somewhere on my right, there's a growl. Something crashes to my left, toward Nyx. She makes a sound of impatience a moment before the sound of hoofbeats fill the room.

The fog invades my nose, licking its way down my throat and clogging my airways. The sound of my own gasps for air mixes with howls and growls filling the room. My head swims. I blink, determined to remain conscious. I try to call my powers again.

The front door bangs open, and Nyx shrieks in fury. The fog choking my lungs suddenly begins to recede. I gasp for breath, and as soon as its hold is weak enough, I push my way out of the barrier.

Chaos reigns in Finn's living room. Finn and Helix have their backs to me, fighting off the three Silenci that have managed to wedge themselves into the house.

Beyond them, I see Nyx. She's clinging to the

doorway, being pulled backward by some sort of magical lasso. I can't see who's on the other end, but whoever they are, they've given me the opening I need.

I grab the candlestick from the mantle and leap at where Helix is crouched. At the same moment, Helix lunges, his body rising to meet mine. I'm driven upward, and the movement offers the height I need to clear The Silenci on his other side.

Helix's teeth sink into The Silenci's throat just as my feet land on the floor behind them. I turn to face Nyx, the pointed end of the candlestick aimed at the dark goddess stumbling away from me.

Nyx's eyes widen at the sight of me coming for her. I swing the candlestick and feel the satisfying thud as it hits her skull. She stumbles sideways, and her eyes roll backward, but I can already see her grip on consciousness hasn't quite slipped.

I cock my arm back, ready to deliver a second blow.

Her breath is ragged, but her hand comes up, stopping my next swing with a bolt of magic that drives me backward and clear off my feet.

My ass hits the ground hard, and I wince. Just behind me, Helix continues to dodge and nip at The Silenci, and I roll away before I'm trampled in the chaos.

Shit. This house is way too small for this.

A bolt of fog tugs at my feet. I spring out of the way as a flash of light splits the sky outside. In the doorway, Nyx shudders then sways, and I finally see who's on the other end of the glowing lasso.

"Aerina!"

"Hurry, Elidi! I can't hold this bitch much longer," Aerina calls back.

I dart out the side door before Nyx can do anything to stop me. The ground is frigid against my bare feet, and I do my best to leap around the small patches of snow still remaining. My black leggings and pink sports bra do little to keep me warm, but I grit my teeth and keep moving.

In the front yard, I spot Aerina struggling to hold Nyx on her magical leash. The Silenci are gathered around her, snorting and shoving against some kind of invisible barrier she's created for herself.

Sweat pours off her skin which is now glowing from the inside out.

She sees me. "Inside the bubble. They can't reach us here."

At her words, several Silenci look up and immediately charge at me.

"I'll deal with them," I call back. "You deal with her."

"What?" Aerina shouts. "No, Elidi, you can't—"

The first demon-horse reaches me, and I use my forward momentum to launch myself around it before it can sink its teeth into my face. I hear the snap its sharpened canines make as I pass its hind legs.

Holy shit, that was close. Too close.

And another one is right behind the first.

In seconds, I'm surrounded by four demon-horses. They've slowed down and are watching me with glowing eyes as they close in around me. My heartbeat thunders wildly in my chest.

So this is how it ends, then. Eaten for lunch by four

horse-demons.

They inch closer, blotting out my view of Aerina, but I don't call out. She needs to focus on Nyx.

One of The Silenci darts forward, its sharp teeth snagging my shoulder and scraping deeply down my arm. Something thick drips from its teeth as it pulls away. I grunt, surprised at the way the bite burns, and realize there's more than just pointed canines threatening me. The Silenci appear to have some sort of acid or poison in their mouths.

I'm surrounded, bleeding, and possibly being poisoned to death already.

A howl splits the air, and my blood runs cold at the high-pitched note it reaches before abruptly quieting. I can't tell whether it was Finn or Helix. Neither one has ever made a sound like that before.

Another Silenci nips at me, teeth out, and I swing, landing a right hook against its snout. It winces and retreats. I do the same with another, then another.

By the time I've landed a hit on all four of them, they've backed away enough to allow me a little space. I start to think I've got this when my right arm goes numb.

Yep, definitely poison. I'm so screwed.

Wings flap above me, and I glance up long enough to see more demon-horses in the sky. My stomach tightens, and I realize the reality of the situation: we're not going to make it. If I'm going down, I'm going to go swinging. My good arm. I square my shoulders and bend my knees into a fighter's stance.

Before I can swing, a bolt of lightning shoots straight up into the sky. I blink, and the boom that accompanies it deafens even the banshee-howls of the monsters before me as the ground shakes beneath my feet.

In the confusion, I cut a path out of my death-circle and run for Aerina.

I spot her on the ground in a heap. Behind me, The Silenci are close on my heels. I can feel their breaths on my neck. One of them gets a mouthful of my hair and yanks. I scream as a chunk of it is ripped away, but I don't stop running. Aerina hasn't stirred, and the bubble of protection that was around her is gone.

She's exposed. We both are.

An energy wells up inside me. Something bigger than the little tricks I've managed so far.

Just before I reach Aerina, I whirl and lift my hand, aiming my palm at the demon-horses behind me. Something hot and wet shoots from my palm. Whatever it is coats the faces of the monsters, and they go crazy, veering away to stomp at the ground and toss their heads as they try to break free. From the weird contraction of their bodies, it looks like they're suffocating.

I fall to my knees beside Aerina and roll her gently over onto her back.

Her face is pale inside the hood of her cloak. Her hair has turned stark white, and she looks aged by at least thirty years.

"Aerina?" I press my fingers to her throat. No pulse. "Aerina, please wake up."

Zeus, Odin, or Whoever you are, if you exist at all, save my aunt.

I shake her like an idiot then remember chest

compressions. Before I can begin, there's a sound behind me. I turn to see Nyx floating over the grass toward us, her mouth curled into evil happiness at the sight of Aerina on the ground.

"Bitch!" I yell.

I climb to my feet and angle myself protectively in front of my aunt. But Nyx barely glances at her.

"She did this to herself, child. Trying to save you, I might add. A pointless attempt."

The energy inside me surges anew. I fling my hand up, and the same liquid from before shoots from my open palm. It hits Nyx in the throat, wrapping around her flawless skin and squeezing.

Her eyes go wide, and she claws at the mystery-liquid now choking her. It solidifies around her skin, and she lets out a strangled gasp. Then she stops struggling and shoots a layer of fog at her throat. Instantly, my magic melts away, and Nyx draws a deep breath.

"Stupid, fucking mortal bodies," she mutters.

I blink at that, confused. "I thought I was the mortal one," I blurt.

She glares at me. "Exactly. A fact that should make all of this so much easier."

She raises her hand. Fog shoots from her open palm, but the shot goes crooked as Nyx is knocked from behind by a big ball of tawny fur.

I scramble sideways to avoid a collision, and the night goddess faceplants into the frozen grass. Before she can move, I shoot her with another coating of whatever weirdo choking goo my body has decided to manufacture. I don't stop until she's completely covered and immobilized from the hardening of it against her limbs.

"Elidi."

My head snaps up, and I look straight into a pair of familiar gray eyes. "Kol." My heart leaps into my throat. "You came."

"I'll always come for you," he says in a rough voice.

Before he can say more, the winged monsters held at bay by Nyx charge straight for him. Kol leaps at them, shifting in midair and coming down again on all four paws. He's a whirlwind of biting and clawing and murder as he tears into two Silenci at once.

Get Aerina out of here!

I don't need to be told twice.

With one arm completely useless, I do my best to drag Aerina awkwardly toward the trees. I'm halfway there when I spot a figure careening toward me at a speed that my eyes can barely track.

I halt, my breath catching at the possibility that Nyx has brought friends to help kill me. But then, I see the low-cut gown and familiar brown braid trailing behind. My belly stirs with attraction even as I mentally roll my eyes at myself.

"Iynx," I say. "What are you doing here?"

"Give her to me." Iynx reaches down and scoops Aerina into her arms.

"Is she—" I can't bring myself to say it.

"She's alive." Iynx runs a hand over Aerina's face and throat, and I watch as something gray is pulled out of Aerina's skin into Iynx's hand.

"I'll take her to my place and do what I can," Iynx says.

"Thank you," I say gratefully.

She nods at me then reaches for my injured arm, letting her hand pass quickly down the length of it. There's a spark, and then feeling returns with a searing pain shooting straight down to my fingertips.

I gasp, shrinking away from Iynx's magic, but she's already done.

"It'll hold for a little while. Then you'll need to get the poison properly removed," she says quickly. Then she shoves me toward Finn's house. "Go. Save the others. Already, I can feel her regathering her power."

With a final parting glance aimed at Iynx then Aerina, I turn and run.

The lawn is a graveyard of Silenci. For a second, the sight of so many of them lying bloody is horrifying. Then a sort of grim satisfaction washes over me, and my eyes land on Nyx. She's still on the ground, but only her legs remain bound.

Something crashes from inside, and I look over to see Helix running for the front door only to be stopped short by a Silenci's massive body suddenly blocking his way. Helix growls and snaps at it, and they both disappear inside, a blur of teeth and claws. Finn follows behind, his teeth bared as he lunges at The Silenci from behind.

I hesitate, wanting to go help them.

Then a wolf howl splits the air, and I spot Kol locked in a morbid dance with two Silenci. His right hip is bloody, and his throat is caked in black liquid. His right back paw hangs weirdly from the joint, and he's hopping rather than walking. He's only barely dodging their attacks now, and I take off at a run for where he's being backed against Finn's truck.

Halfway there, magic hits me, slicing down my spine like an invisible blade. I stumble then go down. At the last second, I twist my body, taking the brunt of the fall on my shoulder instead.

I scramble to sit up. Nyx looms over me, her black eyes blazing in fury. Fog drips from her fingertips and coats her body, already crawling toward me. The first tendrils touch my toes, sending a deeper chill into my bones.

"Bitch," she hisses. "You have been a thorn in my side since the day you were made. But that ends now."

She towers over me, black fog pouring from her mouth onto my skin. It traps me instantly, paralyzing the rest of me with whatever poison it holds. A demon-horse falls hard then slides across the grass, bumping me before it comes to a stop. Its gaping eyes and half-open mouth both leak with the same poison now slowly making its way through my own veins.

I'm too numb to move away. The cold, the poison, and her magic have drained me.

Nyx glares down at me as the fog continues to coat my body.

"Kol," I whisper.

Barely a second later, a blur of sandy-white fur crashes into the dark goddess, and they both go tumbling. The fog curling around me doesn't budge, but it does stop thickening. I struggle against it, gritting my teeth in an attempt to lift my arm. My fingers twitch, but that's as far as I get.

I can only sit, immobile, and watch as Kol's teeth sink into Nyx's arm. She cries out and claws at him, her nail digging into the open wound on his hip. He howls and twists away before doubling back, but the limp slows him down, and she dodges him easily, her magic carrying her out of his reach.

The fog around me tightens into a squeeze, stealing my ability to breathe as she focuses on Kol.

She's playing, I realize, with both of us. Toying with us until she finally tires and kills us both.

The energy surges inside me, heating at the thought of Nyx getting her way, and I strain to reach my magic. It's there. Boiling inside me. I can feel it. I just pray it'll be enough.

With a final, gasping breath, I raise my good arm and shoot.

CHAPTER TWENTY

WITH a sizzle that burns through the condensation hanging in the air, a ribbon of black fire shoots out of my hand. It hits my ankle and slices clean through the foggy tendrils holding me down then blinks out.

A blur of gray fur darts by me, snarling. I sit up and watch Helix join Kol's fight against Nyx. Her fog burns patches of fur from their bodies. She laughs as they circle around her, searching for an opening.

There isn't one.

Nyx looks as fresh as ever. Still playing, she begins to wield her fog like a spear. When she stabs Helix in the throat, drawing a thick wave of blood, he whimpers before going down hard in the frozen grass.

"No," I croak. My chest heaves, and I struggle to crawl toward him.

Kol takes over now, hopping around and striking out with his teeth at the night goddess. She stands over him, smiling in a way that leaves no doubt he poses zero threat to her.

My throat tightens, this time in fear as Nyx raises

her hand.

Rather than jump out of the way, Kol stops and turns to look at me. Our eyes meet, and I see the acceptance in his gaze.

An apology laces through my mind. *I'm so sorry, Elly.*

My heart breaks.

"Kol," I whisper.

Nyx smiles. Behind her, a figure moves in the open doorway. A wolf. Dark brown with eyes the color of honey. Finn.

His teeth are pulled back in a silent snarl aimed at Nyx. Blood drips from his jowls. But he looks strong and mostly unharmed and utterly vicious as he stalks out the door toward the night goddess. She doesn't see him until he's almost upon her. Too busy aiming what I'm almost positive will be a killing blow for Kol.

I inhale sharply.

Finn leaps the moment before the magic she has aimed at Kol unleashes. The shot goes wild, missing Kol by several inches as Finn rips into Nyx.

He narrowly misses her throat, instead tearing her shoulder with a snarl that sends a chill through me. There's violence in his brown eyes, sharper and uglier than any version of Finn I've witnessed in the year I've known him.

He rips a chunk of Nyx's flesh off and spits it away then goes back for more.

Something brushes my shoulder.

It's just me, I hear in my mind as Kol rubs his coat along my back in silent comfort.

Helix appears on my other side. They press against

me, warming me.

"Are you all right?" I ask him.

His tongue darts out and swipes down the back of my hand. It's rough and a little wet, and I scrunch my nose, smiling up at him.

Message received.

Nyx screams, shattering the silence, and overhead, thunder rattles the sky. I look back at where she stands bleeding in front of Finn. Her arm is hanging limp, rivers of blood pouring from the hole Finn's teeth left. But despite the pain, she stares back at him, determined.

Finn's eyes gleam, egging her on.

I can feel Nyx gathering her power now. As if to show the rest of us what she can do, storm clouds gather overhead. Black fog swirls at her feet. Columns of smoke fill her outstretched hands, stiffening and lengthening into spears. In her eyes is pure murder.

Finn tips his head back and lets loose with a howl.

One by one, The Silenci still breathing get to their feet. Their movements are slow and forced, but they wander closer to the showdown between Finn and Nyx, their wings twitching as they move.

More Silenci arrive from the sky, dropping out of the clouds and onto the ground. They surround us, and I can feel Helix and Kol tense. Nyx's lips curl in a snarl.

"You've made a mistake, errand boy," she says, and her words drip with loathing. "My army will eat you alive and spread your bones over this frozen wasteland of a planet."

Finn shifts suddenly, standing in tiny shorts.

"You're the one who's mistaken. This army," he

says, gesturing to the monsters pressing in behind him. "They don't belong to you anymore."

Nyx falters. "What?" she hisses.

"They're mine," he says. "Kill the night goddess!"

The Silenci howl and charge.

"This isn't finished," she yells as she turns to run.

With her goddess speed, she vanishes in a puff of black smoke, her raging scream fading into the woods. The Silenci take off after her, their wings lifting them skyward as they pursue their new prey.

I blink at the yard strewn with the fallen demonhorses. Blood coats the small patches of snow, and in several places, the ground is burned and smoking lightly. Beyond that is what's left of Finn's house. Shards of glass litter the front walk, and the empty doorway offers a glimpse of more destruction inside.

My eyes land on Finn who is staring back at me.

Finn walks toward me but stops short when Helix growls a warning at him.

"El," Finn says. His dark eyes are lined with exhaustion, and his shoulders are sagging as he stands before me.

"How?" I say simply.

He holds up his palm, revealing a fresh scar.

"Ruling over The Silenci requires a blood bond."

His brow is lined with sweat, and I realize the bond he's made is taking more than just his blood to maintain.

"I can hold them off you," he says. "You won't have to worry about them anymore. But Nyx is a different story. She'll be back. And you can't be here when she returns."

Kol and Helix shift back.

"He's right. We need to go," Helix says urgently. "Now."

I assess Finn's strained features and shake my head.

"We'll never make it to the portal in time."

"There's another portal," Finn says. "Inside. Aerina created it in case of emergency."

I struggle to my feet and attempt to follow, but my steps are too slow for Helix. He huffs and scoops me up, carrying me the rest of the way.

Kol scowls but says nothing as he limps behind us and follows us inside.

Finn's waiting at the fireplace. When he sees us, he turns to the brick and draws some sort of symbol in the air with his finger. When he's finished, a silvery window appears, offering a brief glimpse of the desert.

"This portal is only going to last about thirty seconds," he warns.

"Where will it take us?" I ask as Helix carries me closer.

"Aerina charmed it so that it'll deliver you wherever she is," Finn says, and Helix stops.

"You had a portal that led to her this whole time, and you didn't tell me?" I feel bitter about this betrayal more than any of the others.

Finn sighs. "It wasn't safe before, El. Not when we didn't know who had her. They could have been waiting for you on the other side. Ready to kill you the moment you stepped through."

"I trusted you. And you just keep lying."

"I saved you, El," Finn pleads. "Can't that be

enough?"

"Sure, thank you for saving me after causing this shit storm in the first place," I say.

His face falls.

"You need to go," he says quietly. "Before the portal closes."

The silver shimmers, and Helix carries me toward it. I glance back to make sure Kol's following. He reaches for me, and I don't even hesitate. I grab Kol's hand and hold tight to Helix as he steps through the portal and straight into Iynx's wall of goo.

Behind us, I hear the boom of thunder that can only mean Nyx has returned. Helix shoves harder into the slime; the thunder ceases, and I know I've left Finn and his betrayals behind.

CHAPTER TWENTY-ONE

AERINA draws a ragged breath then coughs weakly before falling back to the pillow. I bite my tongue to keep from frowning or showing some sign of my worry for her, but she's too perceptive and rolls her eyes when I try to offer her more tea.

"No more," she complains in a raspy voice. "My insides are drowning in that damn stuff."

"Iynx says it'll help you heal," I remind her.

"I've been chugging it for two days, El." Her voice softens, and I know she's trying to cushion the hard truth for me. "If Iynx's tea was going to help me heal, it would have happened already. What Nyx did to me is beyond the scope of a tea, honey."

She's right although none of us have said it out loud yet. Leave it to Aerina to cut right to it.

"We just need to wait a little longer until we can get a healer," I say, but Aerina shakes her head.

"They're not going to come," she says. "Not when the first two were killed trying to get close. Nyx is going to make sure we're trapped here until she can find a way in."

She's not wrong.

The portal we used at Finn's was apparently unique enough to track, thanks to Aerina's magic signature. For two days, Nyx has camped outside the walls of Iynx's wards, trying her damnedest to get inside. So far, she hasn't breached the magic Iynx weaved against her, but it's only a matter of time.

I need a plan.

I need Aerina well enough to run.

"Exactly why you should be building your strength," I remind her and hold out the tea again.

Aerina groans but takes the mug, probably only to shut me up. She sips, her face contorting at the bitterness of the medicine Iynx has brewed, then hands it back.

"It gets worse every time," she mutters.

"I think she added some more herbs to it," I admit.

"Of course she did," Aerina moans.

"She's trying to help," I say, and Aerina attempts a smile.

"I know. And I'm very grateful she's done so much to keep us both safe." She pats my hand. "You're allowed to be angry with me, you know."

I shake my head. "Of course I'm not angry."

She scowls. "Don't you dare hold back because you feel sorry for me. I don't regret wanting to protect you, but I can see I made a mess of things."

I hesitate to say anything, unsure how to respond. She's right. Things are a hot mess. We've covered a little bit of ground since she woke yesterday, starting with the fact that she never told me I was a goddess.

Apparently, she made a pact with my mother about keeping it a secret for my protection. But neither of us has brought up the elephant in the room that is the emotional wreckage caused by my trip to Finn's.

"Where is your guardian?" she asks.

"I already told you. I don't officially have—"

"Horse shit. You might not have taken the bond, but any fool can see Kol Valco is your chosen guardian."

"How can you be so sure?" I ask. "You don't know anything about him."

"During the few times I've convinced you to go shower or sleep, I've had visitors."

"Kol came to see you?"

"He's worried about you," she says softly.

It's getting harder and harder to hold onto my anger, so I've resorted to avoidance.

"He says you haven't spoken to him since you got back," she presses.

"I'm trying to focus on getting you better," I say, and she groans.

"Goddess above, do not use me as an excuse to avoid your problems, young lady. I taught you better than that."

I sigh. "He lied to me."

"So did I," she points out.

"Yeah, everyone seems to like lying to me."

Aerina's eyes narrow then close, and she exhales. "I'm sorry about Finn, sunshine. He fooled us all."

"It's not just the betrayal," I say, refusing to give in to the tears that burn my eyes at the mention of his name. "I still don't understand why he called Nyx only to turn on her in the end."

"His behavior is confusing, for sure. And something I intend to investigate. I trusted him with your life, and while I'm glad he stepped up in the end, the danger he put you in is inexcusable. It's a matter the Eggther take seriously."

"Helix told me Finn isn't registered with the Eggther," I say quietly.

"Yes, I heard."

I take Aerina's hand gently in my own. "What does Nyx have against me?"

Aerina's usually cheerful demeanor is somber as she looks back at me. Her hair is still white, and the lines around her mouth and eyes make her seem more like my grandmother than my aunt.

"I don't know," she says honestly. "My time with her was spent mostly in pain." I wince, but she continues before I can ask her more. "She has a deep hatred for Hemera, so I can only assume they knew each other once."

"My mother?" I ask, surprised.

Aerina nods. "Though if they did, it's news to me."

Before I can speculate about that, the door opens behind me. I turn to see Helix entering with a tray of sandwiches.

"Iynx sends her regards. She's adding a few more layers to the wards and will come by later."

He sets the tray on the table beside the bed and steps back.

I offer him a grateful smile, and his hand falls to my shoulder in a quick squeeze. In the two days since returning, it's been Helix who I've kept close. For once, his lack of need for conversation is a welcome respite, and he's always checking to make sure I'm getting rest between the times I spend caring for Aerina.

"Thank you, Helix," Aerina says, and I can hear the exhaustion in her words. Our short talk has already worn her out.

"My pleasure." He looks down at me then back to Aerina. "Mind if I steal Elidi for a little while?" he asks.

"Please." Aerina waves me away with a lazy hand and yawns wide. "I'll just nap for a while. You two go."

I squeeze her hand then let it go as I rise to follow Helix out.

"I'll be back soon, and we can eat lunch together," I tell her.

"Don't worry about me," she says more firmly now. "Do something fun. I mean it."

I don't answer as I follow Helix into the guest house's living room and close the door softly behind me. Helix wanders to the bank of windows before he speaks. I follow, tense and anxious at the expression he wears.

"Is it Finn?"

No one's heard from Finn since we left through the portal. Even Helix's pack can't find him, and I don't expect they will. Not while he rules over The Silenci. Just as well because when they do, he's going to be in a lot of trouble for what he's done. Despite everything, I still don't know how I feel about that.

"No," Helix says, staring out the window at the empty desert beyond the glass.

"Is it Kol?" I ask, a lump settling in my gut. Even the sound of his name from my lips is enough to send my panic into overdrive.

"No." Helix shakes his head. "I mean, as far as I know, he's fine."

For all my avoiding, Kol's done an even better job avoiding Helix. Apparently, he wants nothing to do with the Eggther who was there for me when he wasn't. It makes me even more mad to know he can't handle someone else stepping into the spot he willingly vacated.

"Then what—?" I begin.

"Nyx is going to get through those wards." His words are so certain that my panic shifts to our safety.

"How do you know?" I ask. "Did something happen? Is Iynx—"

"Iynx is fine," he assures me. "Nothing happened. It's just inevitable. You know she's going to find a way through eventually. Every day we stay here is another day in danger. For all of them."

I nod because he's right, and I've done nothing but berate myself for it. "I just need Aerina to get better," I say quietly. "When she can move, we'll go."

"Where?" he asks, finally looking at me.

I blink. "I don't know," I admit, "But we'll find a safe place—"

"Come to Tegwood with me."

I bite my lip, torn. Kol had been ready to ship me there before I returned home and made a mess of things. The only reason I'd resisted had been to save Aerina. Now that she's back, there's no reason not to go. No reason other than leaving Kol behind.

"You need to ascend, Elidi. Until you do, you're vulnerable in a way that makes it nearly impossible to protect you. Especially against someone like Nyx. If you think The Silenci are bad, you have no idea what she's truly capable of."

The memory of the fog nearly suffocating me makes me tremble.

"You think I don't know that?" I sigh, my temper leaking away as I admit the real fear that's been eating at me. "Helix, what if I'm not what you all think?"

"What are you talking about?" Helix frowns.

"What if I'm not a light goddess?"

"But you are."

"How do you know?"

"Your mother was Hemera, Goddess of Day. Your aunt is Aerina, Goddess of the Morning. Your divine reading was performed at the exact moment of your birth. The divine doesn't lie."

"Could it be wrong, though? Or maybe not tell the whole story?"

"Where is this coming from?" he asks.

I sigh. "When I was facing down Nyx, all her powers were black. Black fog, black bolts of pain. And she's the Goddess of Night, so it makes sense."

"Okay," he says slowly, still clearly confused.

"So if I'm the goddess of light, shouldn't all my powers be, I don't know, white?"

He shrugs. "I guess."

"Then why can I shoot flaming ribbons of black fire out of my hands?" I ask.

Helix shakes his head, clearly at a loss. "I don't know. But if you want to find out, I can tell you that Tegwood is the best place to get answers. It's designed for ascendings to train and discover their gifts."

I don't answer, mostly because he's beginning to convince me, and I don't want to give in just yet. Stubbornness is a bitch.

"We have healers," he adds as if he can read my thoughts. "They can help her."

I stare back at him. "How would we get past Nyx?" I ask. "Iynx says Nyx will sense if we use a portal. She'll read the signature like before and follow us there."

"She's right. Nyx will know where we've gone, but Tegwood is protected. It's warded with magic from Zeus himself from millennia ago and has never been breached. Only ascendings and Eggther are allowed inside. Nothing can get to you there." Something in his gaze flickers and he adds, "It's why Kol wanted you to go. It's the only place you'll truly be safe."

"What about Aerina?" I ask, my stomach tightening as I realize Helix is right; this is my only option now.

"I'll go through first and get a special pass for her," he says. "When they hear that she's sick, they'll allow it. At least until she's well."

I exhale, some of my worry lifting. "What about Kol?" I ask quietly.

"No Vargar will be allowed to pass."

I nod. His answer is what I expected.

I press my lips together and stare out the window, unseeing. Helix doesn't say anything else while he waits for me to decide. He's letting me choose, and even though I appreciate that—the Helix I met before would have followed the rules, my opinion be damned—I hate the pressure. Like everyone's future hinges on me.

My gaze remains fixed on the window, gazing

outside.

Helix is silent so long I wonder if he's left. Finally, he steps up beside me and his hand lands on my back, pressing just hard enough to let me know he's here. I'm not alone.

"Make the arrangements," I say quietly.

"I'll leave now to secure Aerina's passage," he replies softly. "I should be back by morning for you both."

"We'll be ready."

AFTER packing, I find myself wandering inside Iynx's greenhouse despite the stuffy air. Near the center, a fountain trickles softly. I step closer and am shocked to see several tiny mermaids swimming in the water.

One of the mermaids pops her head above water and offers a wave. She's tinier than a Barbie doll, and her friendly smile wins me over. I wave back, and she beckons me closer.

I take a step before a voice stops me.

"I wouldn't do that if I were you."

I jump back as the mermaid frowns then disappears back into the water. I whirl, and my eyes land on Kol standing in the center of the path. His grey gaze locks with mine, and I feel that same connection, the same tugging need to go to him. To be with him. I push that need away and focus on yet another man who has destroyed my trust.

He's blocking the exit, and judging by the way he's

Hum

watching me warily, he knows it.

I take a step.

"I was just—"

"Leaving, I know," he says, but he doesn't move to let me pass. "Iynx told me you're going to Tegwood."

"Kol, I don't want to do this."

"Do what?"

"Have some big blowout before I go," I say.

His eyes narrow. "Then what do you want?"

His words strike a nerve, and I snap.

"What I want is impossible."

"Tell me anyway." His voice is ragged, raw. His dark eyes are pleading.

"Fine. I want for you to have a good explanation for why you ditched me for Vayda. I want to understand why you and Grim kidnapped Nicnevin and delivered her to your stepmother for torture and interrogation even after knowing she wasn't the one who tried to hurt me."

"Elidi—"

"I want to know how you can kiss me then lie to my face, Kol. I thought you were different. I thought I could trust you."

Tears burn my eyes, but I blink them back, furious with him. With myself. With the future.

He stalks toward me, only stopping when we're toe to toe. His scent fills the air around me, clogging my senses. I should move. But I don't. Apparently, I'm a masochist.

"Grim and I took Nicnevin to save you," he says quietly.

"What are you talking about?"

"Grim and I are bound to Vayda."

"How can you be bound to two people? I thought you said you took an oath for me."

"I did," he says and levels a hard stare at me. "I did, Elidi, and I swear I meant it."

"Then how can she—"

"Before I took the oath to protect you, Grim and I . . . Vayda doesn't trust anyone. In her paranoia, she created a bond between herself and her soldiers. Something we're forced to obey. Grim is still connected to her in that way. He can't refuse her orders. Since I took the oath to protect you, it's not like that for me anymore. Still, she's my alpha, and she enforces that chain of command when she wants something from me. Usually, my presence. Or information."

"So she made you come home," I say.

He nods. A lump forms in my throat as I begin to imagine all the things he's not saying about this power Vayda wields over them.

"She wanted to know about the threat against you," he says. "She heard about Nicnevin—"

"How?"

He hesitates then slides his gaze to mine, and there's so much pain and regret swirling in his stormy eyes my breath catches.

"Grim," he says quietly. "They share things through the bond. Information. He can't always stop her from seeing."

"So she saw Nicnevin," I say slowly.

"She wanted to hear the story for herself. She thinks we were trying to fool her."

"Why would she think that?" I ask.

His mouth lifts in a smile that doesn't reach his eyes.

"Because we were trying to fool her," he says ruefully.

I shake my head. "I don't understand."

He sighs. "Vayda is threatened by you. She's been obsessed with you since the moment I told her of my visions and my calling to protect you. She endorsed my oath, even presided over the ceremony, but she doesn't like the idea of my being here with you. Grim thinks she's going to make a play for power against Zeus. We suspect she'll try to use you to do it, so we've been feeding her wrong information about your attackers and your intentions as a goddess."

"This is crazy. Why would she just think she can use me?"

"She controls Grim and me," he says. "And she knows you care about us."

I bite my lip. He's right. And if Vayda knows it and wants to use it, I'm not sure how I can stop her.

"And Grim?" I ask. "When we first came here, he had to stay behind at first to get away from someone. Was it her?"

"He didn't want Vayda knowing he was involved with you."

"Is he still there now?" I ask.

He nods. "He'll stay at Black Peak until Vayda releases Nicnevin. And don't worry. She won't be hurt," he adds.

"Then where will he go?" I ask.

"Wherever she tells him to," he admits.

My chest tightens at the thought of Grim as

anyone's puppet. "You should have told me all of this," I say.

His gaze burns into my own, and his jaw hardens. "I was protecting you. From her. I had to go so she wouldn't come looking here. Trust me, the last thing I wanted to do was leave you alone. I didn't think—"

"You didn't think I'd disobey your order? I don't take orders from anyone. Not even you."

"Fair enough." His dark eyes gleam. "And I know you well enough now not to expect you to."

My mouth quirks.

His expression lightens to match my own then darkens again as another shadow passes over.

"Can you ever forgive me?" he whispers.

My hands tremble a little because in this moment, I realize there was never any question. Aerina was right. Kol is my guardian. There's no use trying to deny that anymore.

"Of course I forgive you, Kol, I—"

I'm silenced by Kol's mouth pressing roughly against mine.

I go still underneath his touch, then his lips begin to move over mine, I melt against him. His arms come around me, pulling me closer, and my hands slide up his broad chest and hook around his neck, my fingers tangling in his messy hair.

Every nerve ending in my body tingles, and I can't even bring myself to feel embarrassed about the sounds I'm making or the way my body arches up and into his. Anything to get closer. To feel more of this.

My head swims, and I wonder if it's possible to get drunk from kissing. Kol's tongue slides along my lip, coaxing its way inside, and my knees wobble. His arms tighten around me, holding me up as he deepens the kiss even more.

My brain goes deliciously blank, and the dark, empty places in my heart begin to fill with whatever this is. I decide not to define it, especially when there are more interesting things to do like tangle my tongue with his, but one thing is undeniable: Kissing Kol Valco takes me to a realm all its own.

Finally, he eases back, his hand cupping my cheek as he studies me. He's standing close enough that I feel his breath on my face, and I have to press my lips together to keep from hauling myself right back up to that mouth of his.

"No more," he says, his voice ragged.

"No more what?" I ask, breathless. I ease off my tiptoes and feel his hardness brushing over my belly as I move. It distracts me.

"No more leaving." His thumb strokes my cheek, but I shake my head at his demand. His dark eyes plead with mine, and he looks absolutely tortured as he adds, "I can't lose you."

"Because of the bond?" I ask honestly.

He shuts his eyes and shakes his head. "No, Elly. Because of *you*."

My heart skips a beat, and when he opens his eyes again, I can't help the soft smile that's settling on my lips now.

"Are you saying you like me?" I ask, and it's the silliest question after the kiss he just laid on me, not to mention the more important things like almost dying, but I have to know.

He laughs and brings his other hand up to cup both my cheeks. Then he leans in until we're almost nose to nose.

"Yes, Elly. I like you. Not because of the bond we share. Because you're you. I'm sorry I tried to send you away, and I'm sorry I had to leave. I won't do it again."

I nod, and his calloused palms slide back and forth against my skin as I move my head up and down. My gaze catches on his mouth still hovering so close to mine, and my body strains closer, wanting more of him.

"Elly," he groans. "We're in a greenhouse. Not exactly the most romantic spot for this."

"Are you kidding?" I grin, sliding my arms mischievously around his neck. "There are real, live mermaids in that fountain, and that rose over there might be the same enchanted flower from Beauty and the Beast. I don't know a single girl who wouldn't find this place romantic."

He stares back at me with hooded eyes, and his hands drop from my face to my hips. I slide closer, and he guides me perfectly against him until I can feel his length pressing against me once again.

"I can't argue your point," he murmurs, his lips brushing softly over mine this time.

I make a small sound that has his hands tightening around me. He deepens the kiss then stops long enough to whisper in my ear.

"Promise me," he says, pressing soft kisses to my throat. "Promise me we won't separate again."

"I promise," I whisper back, my heart pounding as he seals it all with the best kiss of my mortal life.

CHAPTER TWENTY-TWO

KOL is already awake when I roll over. Our shared blankets are tangled around my legs, and he's propped on an elbow, leaning over me with a crooked smile and bedhead hair. I reach for him, any remnants of sleep instantly chased away by the sight of his naked torso within touching distance. He leans down and presses his mouth to mine in a heated kiss that stirs all my important parts—and even some nonessentials too. I loop my arm around his neck and pull him on top of me, giggling when his kisses turn playful against my neck.

"Did you sleep all right?" he asks against my ear.

"I slept so well I'm thinking about giving up mattresses altogether," I tell him.

"Oh? You enjoyed the floor that much?" he asks, nipping at my ear.

"I enjoyed being caught between the floor and your naked body," I tell him.

He blows in my ear, and I laugh, wiggling away.

The door to the guest house opens then closes, and

a second later, I hear a groan.

Kol sits up, and I lift onto my elbows to see Helix scowling at us both from the other side of the couch.

"Get a room," he mutters.

"We have a room," Kol says cheerily.

"It's being used by the patient," I remind him, nodding at my closed bedroom door where Aerina's still resting.

Helix sighs extra loud, but his eyes skim over my body covered only in a blanket.

At Helix's perusal, Kol's expression hardens.

"You mind?" he snaps.

Helix turns around and crosses his arms, waiting.

I scramble up and pull on an oversized pajama shirt then do my best to smooth out my hair. Kol leans down and plants a quick—loud—kiss on my mouth. Then we both straighten to face Helix.

"Ready," I announce.

Helix spins, eyeing both of us warily.

"How'd it go?" I ask, dropping to the couch and doing my best to ignore his judgy eyes.

"Fine," he assures me.

Kol goes to the kitchen with the tray of dinner we abandoned last night in favor of each other. Helix takes advantage of the space to wander farther inside the room.

"Looks like a lot happened while I was gone," Helix says.

Kol strides over and hands me a glass of water.

"Looks like," Kol says in a voice I know is meant to irritate.

Helix just draws in a long breath, and I wonder if

he's doing a mental count to ten or something.

"You ready to go?" he asks me.

"Actually, I'm going to stay," I tell him.

"What?" Helix's brows crinkle, but he shoots Kol a look that says he knows exactly where this is coming from.

"I've chosen Kol as my guardian," I say. "And I'm not leaving his side again."

Helix stares down at me so long I fight the urge to squirm. Heat burns my cheeks, and even though I don't owe Helix anything, I duck my head, unable to meet his eyes.

The silence stretches on, and I feel Kol's hand drop to my head, smoothing my hair.

"Kol, can you give us a minute?" I ask.

"Sure." He presses a kiss to the top of my head, and I can tell from the way Helix's expression tightens the kiss was a message.

I roll my eyes then offer Kol a reassuring smile as he slips out.

When we're alone, I look up at Helix, searching for the right words. I don't know why, but it matters that I've hurt him just now. His expression has become stony and distant.

I reach for his wrist and tug him down next to me on the cushion.

"Helix, I want you to know how much I appreciate—"

"Kol is in."

Helix's words are so unexpected, my jaw drops.

"What?" I say.

"Kol is in," he repeats. "I pulled a few strings,

which wasn't easy, trust me. I owe way too many people favors for this." He grimaces, which lets me know he's not happy with the prospect of what he's promised. But he looks me right in the eye and adds, "Kol can come with us to Tegwood."

I throw myself against him in a tight hug. He rocks back with a soft grunt. A second later, his arms come around me tentatively, and he hugs me back.

"Thank you," I tell him, squeezing tight.

"You're welcome," he says against my hair, and there's amusement in his tone. Or maybe even pleasure.

"Does that mean I owe you a favor?" I ask.

Helix's lips curve slightly. "Would that be so bad?"

"Not even a little," I say with a smile.

"I already spoke to Iynx about creating a portal for us. We can leave whenever you're ready. The sooner the better so that we can get Aerina to the healer."

The mention of Aerina does wonders to refocus my brain.

"Is Iynx up for that?" I ask.

According to the others, creating a portal inside the barriers Iynx is using to block Nyx is a delicate and draining thing. Besides the strength it would take to balance the two, Iynx has been shut up in her room since we got back, too upset about Nicki's interrogation to come out.

"Kol promised her Grim will stay with Nicki and keep her safe until Vayda releases her. In exchange, she'll create a portal to let us go."

I make a mental note to kick Vayda's ass on behalf of Iynx someday.

"I can be ready in an hour," I say.

He begins to rise, but I grab his wrist again.

"Helix."

He sits again, and I bite my lip as I try to figure out how to ask another favor when he's already done one so big.

"What is it?" he asks.

"I don't want to hurt anyone," I say quietly. "Like with the fire. I burned Grim once before, and I'm just afraid that if I start training with my gifts again, I'll hurt someone else. I don't know if my gifts are as pure as you all think. You swore an oath to protect me, and I know Kol wants you to take it back. And maybe you should since I chose him, but . . . Do you think you could use your oath—just while we're in Tegwood—to protect me from myself? Or protect everyone else from me? Just until I figure this out?"

I half-expect Helix to brush off my worries as silly or stupid or even reject me outright, considering I've officially chosen someone else as a guardian, but he doesn't do either. Instead, he nods slowly, his expression solemn.

"I might have made my promise before my clan and before the gods, but my oath is to you, Elidi, first and last. That means protecting you from all threats including yourself. I'll make sure no one gets hurt if you promise not to hold back and try to ascend. Deal?"

Our gazes lock.

"Deal," I say, and something that's strangely and intrinsically a part of me clicks into place.

Whatever waits for me in Tegwood, I'm not afraid. With Kol on one side and Helix on the other, I'm ready to do whatever it takes to ascend.

I hope you enjoyed Goddess Ascending!

Goddess Claiming (Gods & Guardians #2)

Coming Soon!

About the Author

Heather Hildenbrand was born and raised in a small town in northern Virginia where she was homeschooled through high school. (She's only slightly socially awkward as a result.) She writes romance of all kinds with plenty of abs and angst. Her most frequent hobbies are riding motorcycles and avoiding killer slugs.

Get a complete list of Heather's titles on her website: www.heatherhildenbrand.com.

Other titles by Heather Hildenbrand:

Remembrance: She's the cure that could save him... if only she could remember how. "Witches, Werewolves, and WTF?!"

A Risk Worth Taking: A New Adult Contemporary Romance with southern charm and a hippie farmer capable of swoon and heartbreak in the same breath.

Imitation: A Young Adult SciFi Romance with life or death choices and a conspiracy so deep, even a motorcycle-riding bodyguard can't pull you out.

O Face: Is Summerville's most eligible bachelor hot enough to melt the ice princess herself?